# HOMETOWN HERO

LIBBY HOWARD

# CHAPTER 1

"They're going to drown," Judge Beck commented, the amusement in his voice making it quite clear that although he did believe that his two children were going to wind up in the river, they were hardly going to drown.

We were sitting outside under the gazebo, iced tea in hand as we watched Madison, Henry, Sean, and Chelsea work on their entry for this year's Locust Point Regatta. My boss, J.T., had originally declined to enter, claiming that between business and his YouTube channel reality show, he didn't have the time to build a boat. There was a lot of publicity in having an entry, though, so when I suggested that the kids might be willing to do all the work if he footed the bill, he'd jumped at the offer. 'Boats' could be created using scrap parts taken from actual boats, but couldn't have more than three hundred dollars' worth of materials in them. This made the race one huge comedy show complete with the frantic bailing of water and contestants swimming for shore as their vessels sank. It was part of our town's Fourth of July weekend celebration and had always been a much-anticipated annual event along with the parade, the concert in the park, and fireworks. Local businesses sponsored most of the activities, and town residents took note of those who did, rewarding those companies with their hard-earned dollars throughout the year.

"Dad," Henry called out. "We're going to need more glue."

They were going to need a heck of a lot more glue. I got the idea that most of J.T.'s three hundred dollars was going toward the marine glue and sealant that coated the giant raft. For pontoons, the kids were using huge PVC pipes and chunks of Styrofoam. There was to be a test run tomorrow morning on Suzette Hostenfelder's pond, and I had a bad feeling we'd be dragging a sunken raft out of the water with Suzette's truck.

Judge Beck got up to fetch another container of glue from the garage while I leaned back and enjoyed the view. My hot tub bubbled away at the end of the yard, ready for the kids once they were done with their raft. The herb garden was neat and verdant, little copper signs labeling the different varieties. My roses were just starting to bloom, the flowers actually visible this year now that I'd torn all the weeds and rogue maple seedlings from around them. Taco sulked in the enclosed 'cat run' that the kids had made for him. I felt guilty that he wasn't free to dart around the yard, chasing insects and birds and rolling in my patch of mint, but after Mr. Peter's death nearly two months ago, I hadn't wanted to risk him getting killed himself—either by a sword-wielding murderer, or a car. I felt the cat run was a good compromise to keeping him in the house all of the time, but Taco didn't agree.

Madison and Chelsea came to join me in the gazebo, both girls splattered with paint. They'd been in charge of beautifying the raft and announcing J.T.'s sponsorship, thus the whole thing was a DayGlo shade of pink, with Pierson Investigative & Recovery Services in black on the sides. Thankfully the sponsor's name was long enough that it cut down the eye-watering amount of bright pink.

"Did you hear Holt Dupree is coming back in town for the holiday weekend?" Chelsea asked me, her face flushed with excitement. "He's gonna be in the parade and help MC the regatta."

"Wasn't he signed on to the Falcons?" I asked. "I thought he'd be at training camp or something already."

Holt Dupree was our very own home-grown celebrity. He'd propelled our local high school football team to state four years in a row, starting varsity his freshman year. As impressive as his playing was, no one was surprised when the scholarship offers came pouring in. Of course, a small-town football star didn't always bring in the big names, so everyone *had* been surprised when he turned all of the free-ride scholarships at the b-level schools down to accept a tiny one at LSU. I remember thinking that he was a fool. There were thousands of high school athletes with dreams of a pro career, but few of them ever saw those dreams realized. The odds were good that by his second year in college, he'd be on the bench, taking out a ton of loans to pay for his classes, and desperately trying to figure out what kind of back-up career to choose. The wiser choice, in my opinion, would have been to take the full-ride at a smaller school where he'd be guaranteed play time and could graduate with a degree in accounting and his CPA license.

Holt Dupree proved all of us naysayers wrong. We all followed his games, cheering at each tackle and fumble recovery. By his senior year at LSU, the whole town was buzzing about how he was a real contender on the draft pick lists, and was looking at a big fat contract.

I still think an accounting degree and a CPA would have been a good idea, since athletes can see their careers crash around them with one catastrophic injury, and this year's coveted draft pick can often end up traded away in the spring.

"Yeah, the Falcons," Madison told me. "Third round draft pick. Can you imagine? Right out of Locust Point High School!"

Did I mention that Holt Dupree was a celebrity? Our July Fourth festivities were going to completely revolve around him. The town might as well call the holiday Holt Dupree Day instead.

"He's riding on the high school football float," Chelsea added. "I wish I was a cheerleader so I could be up there with him."

Madison rolled her eyes. "He's twenty-two and has a NFL contract. He's not going to want anything to do with high school cheerleaders."

"Like that's gonna stop any of them from trying." Chelsea flipped her hair back from her shoulder, sticking her chest out. "Oooo, Holt. You're soooooo amazing. Tell me all about that football stuff you do, even though I don't know a wide receiver from a full back. Let me show you my new cheer where I do the splits at the end."

Both girls giggled.

"I don't like jocks anyway," Madison confessed. "Give me a cute nerdy boy any day."

There was a hint of 'the girl protests too much' about her dismissive tone that I recognized. The high school football stars never gave Madison a second look. It was easier to feign disinterest than look like that desperate girl who didn't have a chance.

"Isn't Austin Meadows on the cross country team?" I asked with a smile. He'd taken Madison on a date to a movie a few weeks back. I knew this because her father had nearly had a heart attack over the whole thing.

Madison turned bright red. "That's not the same. Track,

cross country, and soccer guys are cool. They're not jerks like the football or basketball guys."

"How about baseball guys? Wrestling team? Or golf?"

Her eyebrows shot up. "We have a golf team?"

The poor golf team. Those guys, and gals, never got any respect. "Yes, you have a golf team. I highly recommend dating a golf-guy."

"I highly recommend she wait until she's at least twenty before dating *anyone*, even a golf-guy." Judge Beck rounded the corner, a container of glue in hand. "And there's no way you're getting on a float with Holt Dupree even if you suddenly make the cheerleading team."

Madison sniffed. "Dad, he's twenty-two. He's not even going to look at me. And when are you going to stop being so weird about me wanting to go on dates? Are you going to do the same thing with Henry, or is it just because I'm a girl? I'll bet you don't have any problems with him dating girls at fifteen. Not that Dork Face will ever work up the nerve to ask a girl out," she shouted over her shoulder.

"I held hands with Heidi French in third grade," he shouted back. "And asked her to dance at the Teen Mingle last month. By fifteen, I'll be Mister Smooth."

I bit back a smile. The few times I'd seen him in conversation with female classmates, Henry had seemed unaffected by the paralyzing anxiety that struck so many teenage boys. I wouldn't exactly call him Mister Smooth, but he had a relaxed, friendly style that I knew put girls at ease.

Which meant he'd probably wind up in the Friend Zone, as Madison called it.

"Trust me, I will have lots of problems with Henry dating at fifteen. I don't, however, have a problem with him dancing with Heidi French at the heavily chaperoned Teen Mingle. That's very different than being unchaperoned in a dark movie theater. You both are growing up too fast," he

5

complained. "I'm going to put a book on top of your heads to slow you down a bit. Perhaps one of my big, heavy law books."

Madison wrinkled her nose, taking the glue from her father. "I wish you would. I'm taller than almost every boy in my school. I'm even taller than Mom. I hope I stop growing before I reach giant status."

"Well if you see a cake that says 'eat me', don't," I teased. "Clearly you've had too many of those already."

She shot me a puzzled look. Did no one read Alice in Wonderland anymore? It was a sad state of affairs when one couldn't make an Alice in Wonderland reference and expect at least three-quarters of an audience to 'get it'.

"There won't be any boys for me to date if I keep growing," she complained ignoring my cake comment. "They'll all be shorter than me. And if I wear heels, they'll be a whole lot shorter than me."

"Don't judge a man based on size—" Oops. "I mean, based on how tall they are. Date the shorter guys who don't care that you're tall. Those are the ones you want. Those are the guys who aren't intimidated by a statuesque, smart, successful woman."

"Some tall men aren't intimidated by statuesque, smart, successful women," Judge Beck countered. "Or even by average height, smart, successful women."

Was that a compliment? Did he add to his statement reminding me that he was tall and liked assertive women, to add me, a not-very-statuesque woman, into that liked category?

I didn't reply, a bit flustered, and turned to busy myself with the plants I wanted to repot. Madison and Chelsea skipped off with the glue, and Judge Beck turned to me, a wicked glint in his eyes.

"Did you almost give my fifteen-year-old daughter the 'size doesn't matter' speech?"

"Yes. Yes, I did." There was no denying it, although when I'd been talking about size, I hadn't been referring to…that.

He laughed and looked over toward his kids, his expression softening. "They really are growing up too fast. Madison will be sixteen next month, graduating high school and off to college in two years. Then Henry three years after that. I've got only five years left with them."

I made a pffft noise. "You've got a lifetime with them. Instead of children, you'll have a very different, but equally rewarding relationship with them as adults. And eventually you'll have grandkids to spoil and dote on."

"Yes, but only five years of this." He gestured toward the kids squealing and laughing as they waved paintbrushes at each other like they were sabers.

I knew how he felt. It was like a knife in my heart each time I thought of it. Judge Beck would have a lifetime with these two. I only hoped they'd remember that lady they lived with for a few years, and occasionally call or send a Christmas card.

"Cherish this," I said, more to me than to him. "Cherish it and what comes after. All you can do is love how they are today and have faith that there are more good times to come than you'll ever imagine."

"Kay, you are the very definition of an optimist." Judge Beck turned to me with a quick smile, then headed over to assist with the waterproofing efforts on the regatta raft.

A shadow formed over near the hydrangeas, edging closer until it was just off my left shoulder. Eli. At least, what I'd come to think of as my husband's ghost. His presence reminded me of a time when I'd thought all was lost, when I'd gotten that call before dawn and frantically raced to the hospital, still in

7

my pajamas, terrified that I wouldn't get there in time to say 'goodbye'. I hadn't always been an optimist. But sometimes, when life throws a giant curve ball, all a person can do is to hope for better. So that's what I did. Then as well as now.

I set my plants aside, and dusted the dirt from my hands. Today was a glorious day, and I intended to savor every moment of it, as well as have faith that there would be more to come.

"Who's ready for frozen strawberry smoothies?" I called.

There was a chorus of 'me'. Even the judge chimed in. Eli had always loved frozen strawberry smoothies in late June, when it was just starting to get hot and we could sit out on the back porch and sip our drinks in silence, our hands entwined just like Henry and Heidi French in third grade.

"Coming right up," I called out, a contented smile on my lips as I climbed the stairs to the kitchen door.

# CHAPTER 2

The raft sank. Well, it didn't sink right away, but it did eventually sink, slowly taking on water until the kids were squealing and paddling frantically to the shore. Suzette had needed to haul it out of her pond using her truck and a tow rope, which Henry bravely swam out through the murky, muddy water to connect to the sunken raft.

Clearly there was more work that needed to be done, and only today left to do it in. Not that J.T. would mind if his raft sank. In the Locust Point Regatta, winning most definitely wasn't everything. Creativity, humor, and even over-the-top drama in a slowly sinking craft scored a lot of points with us viewers on the shore. This was entertainment. And the most entertaining raft wasn't usually the one that won the race.

Suzette helped us lug the raft back to my back yard and the kids got to work on repairs while I went inside, sliced ham, and made macaroni salad for lunch. Then I headed into the little parlor with my knitting.

The parlor had a new, fairly sizable, addition that meant I'd needed to move furniture around and squeeze the sofa and chairs closer together. Henry had finished his work on the old entertainment console, and found himself unable to sell the monstrosity. His father had swooped in to save the day, claiming to love it so much that he needed to buy it himself. So here it sat, in my parlor, because the only way to get it upstairs to the judge's room would be if we hired a crane and shoved it through the upstairs balcony doors.

After Henry had spent days stripping the varnish off the wood surface, he'd discovered that it wasn't in any condition to be stained. That had left him to decide between a solid coat of paint, or a shabby-chic treatment. With some gentle nudging from me, he'd gone with a distressed look with light green and cream-colored paint that looked like it had worn off and faded throughout the decades. He'd ripped the speaker fabric out and made hinged doors with a diamond-pattern lattice that hid the new Bluetooth speakers. The center section lifted up to reveal a modernized turntable and a USB hook-up. It was a high-tech stereo system in a retro cabinet, and the boy had put weeks of hard work and most of his allowance into it. But for all Henry's knowledge and enthusiasm about antiques, the kid wasn't all that handy with a paintbrush. The entertainment console in the Pinterest picture had been gorgeous. Henry's wasn't.

I loved it. And if Judge Beck hadn't jumped in to buy the thing, I would have myself. I had the same feeling for this entertainment console with the globby paint and lopsided lattice that mothers do for their children's grade-school art projects. I loved every bit of effort Henry had put into restoring it. I loved the happy expression on his face when he'd declared it to be 'done'. He was so proud of his work. And I was proud of him for tackling a difficult project and not giving up halfway through.

So I sat my knitting on the sofa, giving Taco a stern warning not to mess with my yarn, and went over to the console, lifting the lid to put on a Nat King Cole album. It might not be pretty, but the electronics inside were top-notch. *Stardust* filtered through the speakers and I sat down, eyeing the ball of yarn and my hand-written instructions. I had more than enough washcloths. I'd finally mastered the basic newborn hat and had a dozen of them ready to take to the hospital nursery. Now I was ready to tackle something new—a patterned scarf.

I'd attempted The Scarf several times in the past, only to end up unraveling it all. The problem, as my neighbor Kat had told me, was that the only two stitches I knew didn't make for a particularly attractive scarf. She'd given me a simple pattern made up of decreases and yarn-overs that should produce something that looked a lot like the wooden lattice covering Henry's entertainment console's speaker cabinets.

I took a deep breath and cast on the requisite number of stitches, then completed my first row of yarn-overs and knit-two-togethers. The pattern was only 4 rows, repeated until the scarf was the desired length, with rows two and four just a purl stitch all the way across. All I needed to do was to keep track of the pattern on rows one and three, and I'd be good.

By the time the needle lifted and returned on the last Nat King Cole album, I realized that I wasn't good. I'd somehow forgotten the last yarn-over more than once or twice, and my thirty-seven-stitch scarf was now twenty-five stitches. I was going to have to tear it all apart and start over, which seemed to be the way most of my knitting projects went. I wasn't a quick study when it came to this hobby, but like Henry and his entertainment console, I persevered. And in the end I got great joy out of both the process and the finished product, no matter how ugly it might be.

Actually, it *wasn't* ugly, even with the weird shape caused by my inadvertent decreases. Maybe beauty was in the eye of the beholder, but this lattice pattern was quite pretty and the tomato-red silk/wool blend I'd splurged on felt marvelous in my hands. I held it up to my nose, closed my eyes, and inhaled. It smelled like home, like something warm and doughy and soft. I was going to really enjoy wearing this scarf. And that gave me the strength to unravel all the stitches and start again, this time with a background of Sarah Vaughan music.

I joined the kids for lunch, then went back to my knitting and music while they finished the final touches on their raft for the regatta. Then I put together a picnic basket while they showered and got ready for the Fourth of July Concert in the park. The whole time Taco kept me company, and Eli's ghost hovered near, a comforting presence that added to the sense of bliss I'd felt all this day. I loved having this family share my home. I loved knowing they were there, even if I was off in the parlor on my own knitting and listening to music. And I loved hearing the thunder of their footsteps as they came down the stairs, as we all made our way out the doors of my historic Victorian home and into the judge's SUV to head to the holiday concert. Together.

# CHAPTER 3

*S*wann Park was only a few blocks west of downtown and a favorite spot for both picnic goers and joggers throughout the year. A creek winded lazily through the long swath of green, skirting the picnic areas, the playground, the carillon and the concert band shell. Swann Creek flooded with enough regularity that residents could practically mark it on their calendars and remember to move their cars from the street-side parking into the alley behind their houses. Thankfully those homes were set on a hill, so when the overwhelmed sewer system backed up water into the streets, that water seldom made it into the basements of those who lived creek-side.

This evening there was no rain, and Swann Creek was meek and tame, firmly contained by its banks. Instead of standing water, the streets were flooded with cars parked nose-to-tail and people loaded down with lawn chairs, blankets, and coolers.

I would have been one of those people loaded down with lawn chairs, blankets, and coolers, but Judge Beck had taken charge of tonight's outing and I found that all I'd needed to carry was my purse. Henry had two of our four chairs, Madison had the other two, and the judge was dragging our sizable cooler-on-wheels with the blankets tucked under his arm. The lawn around the band shell was quickly filling up, but I saw Matt Poffenberger waving at us and realized he'd secured us a space.

"Daisy and Suzette are joining us," I told him as Henry and Madison set up the chairs. "Will we have room?"

"There's always room." Matt's smile was infectious. "You're still coming to the bingo game after the fireworks, right?"

"Absolutely," I told him as I spread out one of the blankets. Matt spent most of his time at the VFW organizing their fundraisers and events. He was involved in just about every charitable enterprise in Locust Point in some way or another. The late-night bingo game after the fireworks on the Fourth was to help purchase new playground equipment at one of the city parks. I'd invited Daisy and a few others from the neighborhood, turning it into a rare girls-night-out.

"We've got some great baskets for the winners." Matt took the cooler from the judge and wheeled it over next to his own. "I brought some beers to share. Is that okay with the kids here?" he asked.

"The kids are not allowed to have beer," Judge Beck teased. "And I'm driving or I'd drink the ones you brought for them."

"I'll drive," I told him. "You and Matt booze it up. The kids and I will stick with sodas."

"Did someone say beer?" Daisy's voice rang out as she and Suzette made their way to us through the crowd. "Don't you dare let that lush of a judge drink them all."

Matt laughed, flipping the lid on his cooler and making a show of counting the bottles. "I think I can spare one for you, Daisy. And Suzette as well."

"None for me, thanks." Suzette held up a giant bottle of water. "Once again I'm trying to lose some weight."

No matter what the American Medical Association might say, Suzette was not what I would have called obese. She was pleasingly plump with a soft chin, broad hips, and a small stomach roll that occasionally escaped the waistband of her pants and obscured her belt. She also had thick, wavy brown hair that glinted gold in the sunlight, huge, soft, dark eyes, and dimples that creased her round face when she smiled—which was often. I knew her weight bothered her, and it broke my heart because she was such a pretty woman with a kind, giving personality. But it would take more than a sixty-year-old neighbor telling her so for her to believe it.

Matt popped open three beers, passing one to Judge Beck and the other to Daisy, while I dug into my cooler for sodas for me and the kids.

"Dad! There's Chelsea over there. Can I go?" Madison asked, doing a little hop in her excitement. As if she hadn't just seen her friend four hours ago.

"Sure, go ahead." Judge Beck was facing Matt, his back to where Chelsea was, so he didn't see what I did—that Chelsea wasn't over with her parents, but with a group of kids.

And those kids include Holt Dupree.

Holt was holding court. That was the only way I could describe it. He was tall and muscular, dwarfing the dozen nubile teenage girls that surrounded him, and dwarfing nearly all of the six worshipful teenage boys as well.

I wasn't about to rat Madison out, but I cast her a sharp glance, wondering if all her protests about Holt the other day had been the efforts of a girl with a hopeless crush. I remember being critical about guys that I secretly dreamed of but who were totally out of my league. It was a weird sort of self-defense mechanism for teen girls—reject them first before they had a chance to reject you. Although in my case, the dream-boy probably hadn't even been aware of my existence.

Holt Dupree clearly wasn't aware of Madison's existence either. I watched them carefully, noticing how he cultivated his crowd of admirers, but clearly had favorites. He flirted with all the girls, but the ones he seemed to be putting his arm around, or tucking the hair behind their ear, or putting his hand on their shoulder were all of a type—the blonde cheerleader type, in their mid-twenties and model-gorgeous.

Except one. A young woman approached the football star with a wave. She looked to be about his age and was blond, but her looks were more girl-next-door than swimsuit model. She was attractive, but in a very average sort of way— the type of girl it would be easy to overlook, and difficult to remember once she was gone.

Holt obviously remembered her. He looked up at her greeting, and a genuine smile creased his face as he pulled her in for a crushing hug. They spoke for a few moments, Holt ignoring the adoring fans, the far more attractive girls who were not-so-subtly trying to pull his attention from this newcomer.

And then with another hug, and an almost sisterly kiss on his check, the girl walked away, never looking back. Holt watched her for a few seconds, then he turned back to his crowd, once more the football star amid his young adoring public.

"Who's that? She looks familiar, but I can't place her." I asked Daisy, nodding to the young woman making her way past us toward a rusted Honda on the street that looked to be the same age as her.

Daisy turned to give the girl a quick glance. "Oh, that's Violet Smith."

I shook my head, the name not enlightening me one bit as to why I vaguely recognized her.

"Her younger sister is Peony Smith."

"Ah." Peony was a bit of a controversial figure around our home and among Madison's other friends. Her clothing pushed the limits of the school dress-code policy, and she came across as a bit of a wild-child. Judge Beck always seemed a bit uneasy when Madison hung out with the girl. Madison's other friends treated Peony with cool disinterest, but she seemed to be with them often in spite of the luke-warm reception—well, lukewarm from everyone except Madison who truly seemed to like the girl, much to her father's poorly hidden dismay.

And now that my friend had mentioned the relationship, I clearly saw that Peony looked very much like her elder sister. Put them in the same clothing and I wasn't sure I could tell them apart from across the room.

Daisy chuckled. "Seven years apart, but they really do resemble each other. Those Smith girls all look like they were stamped from the same mold. Rose and Gardenia too."

I smiled at the flower names, wondering if Daisy's mother had read the same baby book as the matriarch of the Smith family. The family wasn't personally known to me—well all except for Peony who had been at the house a few times this summer.

"Those girls haven't had it easy," Daisy continued. "Violet managed decent enough grades at the community college to get in at a four-year. She qualified for a few need-based scholarships and took out the maximum in loans, but she had to work almost a full-time warehouse job on the side to help pay for it all. No wonder so few kids rise out of poverty and go to college with those sorts of hurdles."

Daisy's vocation was working with underprivileged youth. She also volunteered at a crisis center that assisted runaways, pregnant teens, and victims of abuse as well as kids battling addiction. She knew everyone in town, especially those who had passed through her doors at some time or another in their lives.

"And you helped her get some of those need-based scholarships?" There were plenty of reasons Daisy might know the Smith girls, but I was going to assume the least troubling of those reasons.

She nodded. "I wish there had been more available."

And that said it all. Churches and other organizations had small scholarships of a few hundred dollars that were happily given each year, but a few hundred here and there didn't go far when tuition as well as room and board added up to nearly as much as these kids' parents brought home each year. Government aid, loans, and these small scholarships only went so far.

"So how does Violet know Holt Dupree?" I asked. She didn't really seem to be his type as far as girlfriends went, but maybe I was being too harsh in my judgement. The boy was putting on a show, acting the part of the celebrity. Who knows what he truly valued in a girlfriend when he was away from the public eye?

"Oh, they grew up together. The Duprees and the Smiths are practically neighbors in Trenslertown."

Trenslertown wasn't really a town. It was a tiny neighborhood that was, quite literally, on the wrong side of the tracks. There was a swath of land between the rail line and the highway, and in that section of land were a dozen or so houses—cinder block, plywood-sided, and clapboard, as well as a few old rusted mobile homes all hidden from view by overgrown briars and vine-choked trees. It was where Locust Point's poor lived, generations stuffed into those drafty homes.

Suddenly that warm greeting made sense. To everyone else, Holt Dupree was a football star, a local boy who'd made it big. To Violet Smith, he was that kid from down the street who'd experienced the same drafty winters and canned-bean

dinners as she had. There was a brotherhood, and a sister-
hood, in those who'd shared the same childhood circumstances. No surprise that he'd greeted her so warmly. Out of
everyone who'd clustered around him, she'd probably been
the only one who really, truly knew who he was beneath the
shine of his NFL football contract.

I turned my attention back to the celebrity. As the band
started their sound checks, I noticed that Chelsea and
Madison had been shuffled to the outer ring of admirers, not
quite making the cut. I was torn between relief and irritation.
Chelsea was adorable, but Madison was stunning with her
dark, sable brown hair and hazel eyes. At almost sixteen, the
girl had blossomed with long shapely legs and a trim, neat
figure just like her mother's. But she was very tall, pushing
close to five foot eleven. There was a good chance she'd end
up at six feet, and in spite of what I had said the other day,
that did intimidate a lot of boys.

I got the feeling it intimidated the even taller Holt
Dupree, who seemed to like the five-foot-two-eyes-of-blue
girls. And as much as his rejection of Madison might smart,
I was relieved. He was twenty-two and heading to Atlanta
for a pro-football career. She was almost sixteen with no
chance whatsoever of holding a young man's attention in a
long-distance relationship, especially when he would most
likely have women throwing themselves at him left and
right.

Besides the fact that she was fifteen, and that sort of thing
would have been frowned upon even if they had remained
chaste. Such a relationship would not have been good for a
young man on the verge of what could be a lucrative professional sports career.

"Is that…?" Judge Beck's eyes blazed and he rose out of his
chair, his eyes focused in on his daughter.

I put my hand on his arm. "I've been watching her. He

hasn't said two words to her the whole time she's been there. Let her be. I guarantee she'll be back when the band starts."

The judge hesitated. I felt the muscles in his arm tense, saw the corner of his jaw twitch as if he were grinding his teeth together. Then slowly he lowered himself back into the seat.

Just as I predicted, as soon as the band began the first set, Madison and Chelsea came back to us, grabbing sodas from the cooler and sitting on the blanket, their heads together as they sang along to the opening song.

I still kept my eye on Holt Dupree. He was moving through the audience like some sort of pied piper, trailing an ever-growing crowd of admirers as he shook hands and kissed babies like a politician. He was garnering just as much attention as the band—more actually.

"I don't like that guy." Matt leaned over, his mouth practically in my ear to be heard over the band.

"Who?" I hoped he could read lips, because I wasn't going to shout into *his* ear.

He jerked his head, and I assumed he meant Holt Dupree, although he could have been indicating any of the dozens of people surrounding the football player. I had to wait until the end of the first set and for the applause to die down before I could ask him why.

Matt glared over at the crowd. "A friend of mine has a son who went to school with Holt—Buck Stanford. Buck played football, and he was better than Holt, but he got clipped after the play and tore his ACL. He had to sit out his junior year, which is when all the college recruiters come to check out the high school players."

I waited, thinking that there had to be more to the story. I doubted Matt would dislike someone based on a friend's son's jealousy.

Matt turned to face me, and the expression on his face

chilled me. "The hit that tore his ACL wasn't from someone on the opposing team, it was another Locust Point High School player. It all looked like an accident with a big pile-up going for a fumble, but the kid who injured him was Holt Dupree."

"But if there was a pile-up, how did he know it was Holt?" I asked. "And how did he know it wasn't an accident? Kids, and adults, get hurt in football all the time."

I knew next to nothing about football. Yeah, I loved going to the Friday night varsity games, and I knew enough to follow what team had the ball and when there was a touchdown, but beyond that I was clueless. I'd been that nerdy girl in high school who dated the chess club guys, and neither of my parents had been the type to watch Monday night football. Even when Eli and I had hosted Superbowl parties, I spent more time putting out snacks and watching the commercials than the game.

Matt shook his head. "Nobody saw it, but Buck says it was Holt, and that it was intentional."

I'm sure he could see the doubt on my face. I didn't want to cast aspersions on his friend's son's credibility, but in a pile-up, with all that adrenaline and excitement...it must have been an accident. Or another player from the opposing team.

"Sometimes players have a lot of forward momentum," Matt explained, "and occasionally a hit, a tackle, takes place after the play ends. Referees have to really scrutinize what happened, because sometimes it's truly an accident that's a split second after the whistle blows, and sometimes it's a deliberate attempt to intimidate or disable a player on the opposing team, and cover it up by making it look like an accident."

"That's...that's horrible." I suddenly thought back to all those high school games I'd gone to and wondered if there had been an immoral kid who could deliberately injure another.

"Buck says Holt 'tripped' and fell into him right after the play had ended, and fell in such a way that he kicked Buck's knee. He was a sixteen-year-old kid and he needed surgery and physical therapy. By the time he recovered enough to play, the season was over and so were his chances at a scholarship opportunity."

That was horrible—if it was true. I trusted Matt, but I got the impression he was one of those incredibly loyal guys who always backed his friends. And it would be very hard for a man whose son had been injured, who'd lost out on a huge, life-changing opportunity, not to see intent where there was none.

Holt Dupree seemed to be every stereotype of a good-looking football player, but that didn't make him the sort of guy who would deliberately injure and ruin a teammate's chances.

Nothing I could say would change Matt's mind on this, so instead I made a sympathetic noise and patted his hand. "What's Buck Stanford doing now? I'm assuming he went to college even without the scholarship?"

Matt nodded. "Two years of community college, then he finished this year with a degree in business from the state university. He's back in town, in Milford, working at his dad's company."

Stanford. I searched my memory. "Stanford Paving?"

"Yep." Matt grimaced. "Stu's really counting on winning that contract with the state for the work on I-95. Put in a prayer for him, because he really needs that contract."

I wasn't exactly the person to turn to for prayers, given that I rarely went to church, but I promised to put in a good word for Stanford Paving, and turned to listen to the band's second set.

By the third set, Holt Dupree and his followers had made their way to us. At the band break, they burst into our little group with all the finesse and welcome of a swarm of ants at a picnic.

No, not ants. They were like those religious evangelicals knocking on your door at dinner time, forcing their way into your house to tell you the Good News about Holt Dupree.

Then just as quickly as he'd blown into our midst, he'd left, picking up Henry, Madison, and Chelsea in his wake.

And Daisy.

I blinked in surprise when my friend got up and headed after the gaggle of teens and twenty-somethings following the football player, but when she turned to me with a wink and a grin, I knew what she was up to.

"Daisy's on it," I told Judge Beck. "And trust me, nothing is going to happen on Daisy's watch."

My best friend had dedicated her life to helping at-risk teens. She'd taken every underprivileged girl that came through those doors into her heart, and she did her best to protect them, to make them see that they had choices and opportunities beyond the pile of doo-doo that life had handed them. She'd counseled mothers as young as thirteen, helped fourteen-year-olds kick their drug habit, and held the hand of rape victims as they filed their police reports. Holt Dupree would find himself with a concussion if he so much as laid a hand on one of those girls.

Still, I was very aware of the tension in both men that sat on either side of me. Their eyes followed Holt Dupree everywhere. I could understand Judge Beck, he had a young daughter who had made at least one foolish decision in the past six months, but Matt's concern surprised me. I knew he and Judge Beck had been playing the occasional round of golf together, but I hadn't really thought their acquaintance-friendship was at the level where Matt would be watching out for Madison, especially with her father right here.

Finally, Matt leaned over, his mouth again disturbingly close to my ear. "Buck's in that crowd with Holt Dupree, and I don't see anything good coming of that."

Drat. I looked over at the group and quickly picked out the boy from Matt's description shouted into my ear. Buck Stanford was a few inches shorter than Holt, and looked to be lighter by about thirty pounds, but he was still what I would call 'buff'. For a second I thought maybe the father's resentment wasn't a reflection of his son's, but then Buck turned and I saw his face.

The hate practically rolled off the young man. I winced, agreeing with Matt that nothing good was going to come of this.

Buck followed on the outskirts of the crowd, and as the band finished their last set to loud applause, I lost sight of him. Henry had returned earlier, but with the close of the concert, Madison came racing back, breathless with her hazel eyes sparkling and a rosy glow on her cheeks.

"Dad, oh Dad! There's a party tonight. Chelsea is going and so is Miranda and Babette and Maria. Can I go? Can I go?"

There was a world of information in the lack of information Madison had conveyed. I knew this, and so did Judge Beck. His jaw set and one of his eyebrows raised as he regarded his daughter.

"Where is this party? And who is chaperoning it?"

Madison's face fell. "Persimmon Bridge Park. I promise that I won't drink any alcohol. Lots of adults will be there, too."

"Like Holt Dupree?" the judge asked.

She flushed a bright red. "He's an adult. And so are his

friends. Please Dad? Chelsea is going. And Miranda, Babette, Maria, and Peony."

I could immediately see that the inclusion of Peony Smith in this party did nothing to advance Madison's case. Judge Beck was a very fair man, and I'm sure in his courtroom he would never harbor assumptions about someone based on where they'd grown up or the circumstances of their life, but he was also a father. And as unfair as it was, a father sometimes didn't want their child hanging out with a girl whose family included those with drug and alcohol addictions, criminal records, and a history of teenage pregnancy.

"No, Mads. You're not allowed to attend this party."

"Dad!" the girl wailed. "There won't be any drinking or anything. And all of my friends are going."

"I can pretty much guarantee there will be alcohol at a party hosted by Holt Dupree and his friends," Judge Beck announced. "No. You're not going."

"I won't drink any," Madison pleaded. "I swear I won't drink any alcohol. Please, Dad!"

"No." There was the weight of finality in that one word.

Tears sparkled in Madison's eyes and she spun around to hide them from her father. I gave her the privacy she needed and helped pack up the drinks and blankets, handing Henry the extra chairs. I said my goodbyes to Matt and Suzette then fell back to walk with Madison as we made our way to the car.

"I'm sorry honey," I told her. "Before you know it, you'll be an adult and going to whatever parties you want, but for now try to respect that your father only has your best interests at heart."

"He invited me," she choked out. "He actually smiled at me and asked me to come to the party. I'll never get a chance like that again."

I looked back at the young celebrity in question and halted. Holt's crowd of followers were standing back a safe distance while he and Buck Stanford were engaged in what was quickly becoming a shouting match. Then with surprising speed, Buck's fist shot out and nailed Holt in the face. The crowd closed in, obscuring the fight and I turned around to catch up with Madison and the others, hoping that she was right and that she'd never get the chance to party with Holt Dupree again.

# CHAPTER 4

"*W*here'd you run off to after the concert? Should I worry that you've fallen victim to Holt Dupree's charms?"

Daisy sniffed, relaxing into her child's pose. "Right. Like he wouldn't notice a fifty-five-year-old woman hanging out at his party at Persimmon Bridge Park, drinking beer from a red Solo cup and trying to blend in with people less than half her age."

"I thought maybe you'd decided to give the cougar thing a go," I teased.

"Like Kari Macintosh?" She snorted. "Hardly. I followed them around a bit at the concert, taking note of who he was paying special attention to and who seemed to be actually friends of his instead of just hangers-on."

"And?" I urged. Daisy was just as much of a snoop as me. I was dying to know what the aftermath had been in the fight between Holt and Buck as well as who might be getting cozy with our local celebrity. Just as long as it wasn't Madison or any of her young friends.

"You know, the guy is really charming." Daisy stood into a

Vriksasana, and I did the same. "He's arrogant as all get-out, but charming. I guess I'd be arrogant too if I'd just scored a major NFL contract, though. He's not dumb. He's chummy with all the guys—even the young boys who came up for autographs. He makes them feel like they're really something special, not just a fan pestering him when he wants to be left alone. The guy can really work a crowd. If he can stay injury-free, he'll land a ton of sponsorship contracts."

I thought of Madison and how her aloof I-don't-care-about-football-guys had done a one-eighty last night. "And the girls?"

"Every one of them gets special attention. He remembers their names, and flirts just enough to get them all giddy without crossing a line. He seems careful to keep anything that might be sexual-innuendo to those who are clearly his age or older."

"See? You've got a chance with him."

She laughed. "Not that much older."

"I'm still glad Madison didn't go to that party. Judge Beck stayed up late and actually left his bedroom door open last night. I think he was worried that Madison might try to sneak out." I focused on the horizon, trying to hold my tree pose with the same level of balance as Daisy.

"After the grounding she got from going to that party with Chelsea? I don't think she'd try something like that."

I mirrored Daisy's transition into a chair pose. "You said yourself that the boy has charisma. Madison's at a tough age. She's so tall and she's comparing herself to the curvy petite blond girls that are getting the boys at school, and feeling insecure. Holt asked her personally to come to the party. Think about it. A hot grown-up guy who is going to be playing for the NFL this fall looked her in the eyes, smiled, and asked her to come to this party. What would you have done?"

"Me? I would have made a rope ladder out of my bedsheets and been in Persimmon Bridge Park before they tapped the keg," Daisy replied. "But from the outside looking in, I saw that Holt Dupree asked every single girl and boy at that concert to the party. Like I said, the guy has some serious mojo going on."

I sighed. "Well, he'll be gone in another two days and I doubt he'll ever be back to this little town again."

Daisy slid effortlessly into a half-moon pose. "Which means you'll need to deal with a sulky teenage girl for the next two days."

I wobbled, dropping my upraised leg a bit lower for stability before I replied. "Possibly longer than two days. Chelsea, Maria, Babette, Peony, and Miranda all went to that party last night. It's going to be salt in the wound because they'll be rehashing the excitement for months."

Daisy shot me a sympathetic glance. "I saw that a couple of my mentees were going. I'll ask them today what went on there."

"Probably underage drinking, and making out." I commented wondering if Holt had kept everything strictly professional, or if he'd decided to take one of his admirers home with him. I wasn't sure what set me off about this guy. I'd read about his skill when he was part of the local high school team and hadn't really thought twice about him before this week. What was it about his celebrity status that bothered me?

I thought of Madison, and had a sudden flash of self-awareness. I'd never attracted the attention of the football players either. If I'd been fifteen, I doubt Holt Dupree would have even bothered to ask me to that party. I probably would have been invisible to him. And I'm sure *that* was my issue with the young man, not any of his actions. Outside of what Matt had alleged, I could see that Holt had done nothing wrong. He'd been very savvy about taking a talent and using it to get ahead, and with his friendly demeanor and looks, he was ensuring that even after that talent faded, he'd have established himself as enough of a name to continue to ride the success the rest of his life. There was nothing heinous about that. It was smart business—far more savvy than I ever would have expected from someone who was only twenty-two.

"Madison kinda sealed her fate when she said that Peony Smith was going," I commented, grateful that we were winding down into a hero pose. "I get the feeling Judge Beck isn't a fan of hers."

Daisy grimaced. "Peony Smith's main crime is being born poor."

"She does have a reputation for being a bit wild." At least that's how it seemed to me from Madison and her friends' conversations.

"That's a whole other story. Kids like her have little parental supervision. They grow up in neighborhoods where illegal activity is the norm, and in her case, two out of three of her sisters isn't the best role models. It's a wonder she's still in school with no criminal record."

"That bad?" I had no idea what her family life was like, only that kids from Trenslertown usually didn't have much in the way of opportunities.

"Yeah, that bad. Although the only 'wild' I've heard of Peony Smith is that she parties and tends to be less than discriminating when it comes to alone time with other boys."

I winced. "That's probably what the judge worries about. He doesn't want Madison hanging out with kids who are out until two in the morning drinking and making out with equally inebriated boys."

We finished off with an appropriately named corpse pose, then Daisy stood and helped me to my feet. "The drinking is a problem, but it drives me nuts how girls get shamed for the exact same behaviors that everyone celebrates in boys."

I nodded. "Why as much social pressure isn't put on boys to remain celibate, I'll never know."

"The trend is going the opposite way from celibacy for both boys and girls," Daisy replied as we headed to my kitchen and the lovely siren song of fresh brewed coffee. "There's pressure to not be 'uptight', and there's a sort of cool factor now about having sex early."

"I'm sure our grandparents lamented the same way over our morals," I told her. "Not waiting for marriage. Letting boys kiss us goodnight on the porch. Good heavens!"

"And you'd get a reputation if you were one of those girls who French kissed," Daisy complained. "I don't think kids now even know what French kissing is."

"That's because it's all French kissing. Anything closed mouth is chaste, like you're kissing your grandmother or something."

I liked chaste kisses. They were soft and tentative, or lingering and filled with promise. There was something to be said for a slow courtship instead of tumbling into bed a few hours after you'd met. Although maybe I was just being nostalgic. Eli and I had certainly hurried things along, but back then 'hurried' had been after six or seven dates. Ugh. Was I turning into one of those old women who forgot what it felt like to be on fire for someone? I hoped not.

Daisy sighed. "If only French kissing were the worst thing I dealt with each week. I swear working with teenagers is the most challenging thing I've ever done. That stage of their life… it's like sending them down a hall with slamming gates and spinning knives. I breathe a sigh of relief every time one makes it out alive, or clean and sober, or not pregnant."

I thought again of Madison and how lucky she was. "So many of them don't have the best parental role models. For all the divorce nastiness, I think Judge Beck and Heather are doing a good job."

"Madison *is* lucky. But then you get kids that manage against all odds to pull themselves up out of the hole, like Violet Smith." Daisy shrugged. "Sometimes it takes more than good parenting. Kids fall in with the wrong crowd, or get their hearts broken, or suffer from undiagnosed mental illness. I've seen exemplary parents shocked at how their child managed to hide an addiction from them. Sometimes I think it takes luck to survive."

I nodded in agreement. "Luck or divine intervention."

# CHAPTER 5

*J*.T. had set up an elaborate spread for his 'VIPs' on the banks of the Piwa River for the regatta. There was a pavilion with chairs and a buffet table that held elegant sandwiches with the crusts removed as well as chips and other less high-falutin fare. I'd done a double-take as we arrived, wondering if guilt over his lack of involvement in his company's raft entry had spurred him to put on such a spread, but then I realized what his motive was the moment Daisy appeared.

His face lit up. Next thing I knew there were champagne corks popping. Oh Lord, this was all my fault. I'd made a joke one day about Daisy's interest in knife rests, and my boss had totally misconstrued the comment. Now he was crushing on my friend like he was back in high school.

Daisy had turned up her nose at every mention I'd made of J.T., but the moment the man broke out the champagne and the plastic, fake-crystal flutes, herded her to the best seat for viewing, and raced back and forth with sandwiches and cocktail wieners like a waiter, I realized my error. As quirky

33

and feminist as my best friend was, she liked to be wooed. Inviting her to be an actress in his unpaid YouTube series hadn't done it. A million hints about how he should be invited to dinner hadn't done it. This might just do it. Daisy was in her element, daintily munching on a sandwich that looked like something the Queen of England would eat at a polo match, while holding expensive bubbly in the other hand. I was pretty sure all of this had bumped J.T. up a few notches in her very selective evaluation scale.

It made me wonder once again what was in their past. Daisy had known J.T. before I'd taken a job with him. She'd hinted that she'd known him for a good part of her life. And from the snark, the eye roll that happened every time she talked about him, I'd gotten the feeling there had been something there once—something that hadn't completely vanished.

But that was none of my business. I could gently pry. I could hint and nudge. But at the end of the day, if my best friend didn't want to confide in me, then I'd accept that. In the meantime, I smirked and kept my thoughts to myself as she lorded it over we peons, soaking up my boss's attentions while the rest of us got situated and awaited the start of the race.

Judge Beck was with our group, as were Suzette, Carson and Maggie, Kat and Will Lars, Bert Peter, Bob Simmons, Jeanette and Paul Tennison, and Deanna, the judge's paralegal, with her husband Steve. I waved over Reverend Lincoln, and Matt Poffenberger who were both roaming the banks with their lawn chairs, looking for a spot.

"Your father couldn't make it?" I asked Matt as I snatched the chair from his hand and sat it next to mine.

He sighed. "Dad is having a rough day. I came by this morning to pick him up, but it just wasn't going to happen. I hate that he's not here. He hasn't missed the regatta since he was a kid. My only consolation is that he'll never remember he couldn't come."

Matt went off to help himself to the buffet, only to have his chair moved aside as Judge Beck scooted it over and plopped his own chair in its place. He had two champagne flutes in his hand, one of which he handed to me.

"I'm only drinking the one," he told me. "I'm pretty sure I'll need to dive into the river and rescue my kids, so I better be sober."

"I believe I've seen both of your children swim," I commented. "And I think the five gallons of marine sealant they put on that raft should be enough to keep it afloat."

"I have my doubts," he drawled. "But so far, so good. We got it off Suzette's truck and into the water without any disaster. It seems to be floating for now. We'll see how it does with four kids standing on top of it."

The starting gun went off and the crowd all stood cheering as the rafts came into view. Hoskins Real Estate was in the lead, three middle-aged perfectly coiffed blondes paddling in a steady rhythm. Close behind them was the Farmer's Coop team and Dial's Pizzeria. The Fischer Plumbing team was already sinking fast and bailing with all their might. There was a shout, and the crowd erupted into cheers and laugher as the plumbers' giant modified bathtub capsized, dumping them all into the water.

The announcer read off their names for the Wall of Shame and we cheered again as the men emerged dripping wet onto the shore. The pack of rafts began to thin out as the more seaworthy ones pulled ahead, and I caught a glimpse of our boat.

"There!" I shouted, jumping up and sloshing my champagne over the edge of the glass. "Look, they're still afloat."

They were, paddling like crazy with the girls up front and the two boys in the back. It took me a few seconds to register that there was a fifth figure in the boat—a tall dark-haired boy with broad shoulders and muscles on muscles.

I caught my breath and out of the corner of my eye, saw Judge Beck stiffen.

"What's he doing on their raft?" he demanded. "When I left them, he wasn't there. He's supposed to be announcing."

Someone else was clearly announcing, and it was just then that someone started to make a big deal about Holt Dupree on the Pierson Investigative and Recovery Services raft. It was all so awkward. This would definitely give J.T. some added press and promotion, but I knew Judge Beck was furious.

Of course, the question in my mind was 'why'? Why was Holt Dupree on a raft with a bunch of kids—these kids in particular? And why was Judge Beck so upset? Did he know something about the charismatic young man that I didn't?

"Chelsea was at that party last night," I commented. "Maybe she invited him to be on the boat. It could be a completely innocent publicity stunt. He'll get more press paddling with four kids than in the announcer booth."

"Or maybe Madison invited him." The judge narrowed his eyes as Holt skimmed his oar along the water and splashed the two girls. They both squealed. The boys laughed. And suddenly a race for twelfth place became a water fight in the middle of the river. The Hoskins ladies and the Coop were battling it out for the lead, but everyone's attention, and the announcer's as well, were on Holt Dupree and the kids as water flew, the teens laughed, and the raft rocked perilously from side to side.

Holt swung his paddle, and water drenched Madison, who retaliated. The football player ducked, and Henry jumped to avoid getting even wetter. It was too much weight on the right side of the raft. The whole thing lifted up, and with a chorus of screams, overturned.

I heard Judge Beck catch his breath as he set the glass of champagne aside and readied himself to dive in after his kids, but it wasn't necessary. Five drenched heads popped up in the water, laughing and sputtering as they swam toward the shore. Holt got to the shallows first, standing, then turning around to scoop Madison up in his arms and carry her to solid ground. The crowd was thrilled. Judge Beck was less thrilled. With his hands in fists, he stomped down toward the water. I ran after him, hoping that he wouldn't make the sort of scene that would alienate his daughter. There was time to discuss this with her later. Not now when everyone in the town was looking on, and the announcer was making some inane comment about damsels in distress.

Holt sat Madison down the moment they got to shore, and without so much as a lingering caress, dove back in to do the same to Chelsea. Judge Beck slowed, realizing that although Holt might be a flirt, he wasn't doing anything terribly improper with his daughter. After Chelsea made it to shore, Holt went back and made a joking show out of trying to carry the boys out as well. Henry splashed him off, but the football player managed to grab Sean and haul him to land in a fireman carry.

"It's just a publicity stunt." I tugged on the judge's shirt, trying to get his attention. "Don't embarrass Madison in front of the entire town. She'll never forgive you."

Well, maybe not never, but it would certainly put a dent in her relationship with her father. I wasn't sure if my words made Judge Beck hesitate, or the realization that aside from carrying Madison ten feet through shallow water, Holt wasn't paying her any particular attention. The guy was high-fiving the boys and laughing as he pushed the wet hair off his forehead. Then he yanked his shirt off to yells and whistles, and tossed it into the crowd as he headed up the hill past us to J.T.'s tent.

"Sorry, Mr. Pierson." He grinned and reached out to shake J.T.'s hand. "I think I blew our chance at first place."

A crowd had formed, everyone taking pictures of the shirtless athlete. J.T. beamed.

"I don't think we were in the running for first place anyway," he told Holt. "Those Hoskins women win every year."

Sure enough, the announcer shouted out that Hoskins Real Estate had won their fifth year in a row, in a very close run with the Farmer's Coop. J.T. offered Holt sandwiches and went to get him a bottle of water. The kids joined us. Daisy handed them each a towel to dry off. And we turned to watch the rest of the regatta participants as they slowly sank, or capsized, or struggled across the finish line in their water-logged crafts. Judge Beck was still eyeing the football star with the kind of attention one gives a venomous snake. What the heck was going on? I got that he didn't want his daughter getting in trouble with an attractive, charismatic, older boy, but this seemed personal.

I walked up to him. "Okay, spill it. This is a little overprotective, even for you. What do you have against Holt Dupree?"

"What do you mean?"

I laughed. "Come on. You bristle every time his name comes up, watch him like you expect his head to start spinning around, have a heart attack every time Madison is within twenty feet of the guy—what's going on?"

Just to prove my point, Judge Beck shot the football star another glare. "When he was in high school, Holt Dupree had a reputation. That reputation followed him to college, and there was an incident. Charges were dropped, but judging from how he was as a teen…let's just say I'm concerned."

Well, if that wasn't the most intriguing, vague statement ever. "I'm guessing he was accused of something with an underage girl?"

"Yes." Judge Beck shook his head. "He was twenty and she was fifteen, so it's not like the age gap was all that big. It was down in Louisiana. There was alcohol involved. He claimed she showed a fake ID to get in to the party and that he never touched her. Like I said, the charges were dropped."

"But?" I pressed, knowing the judge knew more than he was telling.

"Who knows what happened? The accuser couldn't pick him out in a line up. Holt had an alibi—he was out in the open with all the other partygoers, then with a different woman the rest of the night. There was no physical evidence."

"I'm a huge believer in giving the victim the benefit of the doubt, but maybe Holt *was* innocent," I said.

"Maybe, but back in high school, the guy went through girls like they were disposable napkins. The daughter of one of my golfing buddies attempted suicide after Holt forwarded around some racy texts and pictures she'd sent him. I don't trust the guy, and I especially don't trust him around my daughter."

I caught my breath. "That's horrible! That poor girl."

"Robert pulled her out of school for the semester, hoping the scandal would die down. He ended up sending her to a private school out of town so she could make a fresh start somewhere."

It made me think of Daisy's and my conversation during yoga this morning. Racy pictures and texts of Holt would have done nothing but made him seem like a stud, someone to be idolized, but for a young girl, the same thing would get her shunned. No wonder the judge was hyper vigilant.

And I couldn't blame him. Madison was a smart, mature girl, but teenage hormones tended to overwhelm even the most level-headed girls, especially when there was a handsome football star smiling at you and inviting you to his party.

# CHAPTER 6

"*J*heard from my sources that the party at Persimmon Bridge last night was quite the hit," Daisy told me with a grin as we repotted geraniums in hanging baskets for my front porch. The kids were off at their friends' houses for the afternoon, and Judge Beck had headed off with his golf clubs for a quick nine. I was drenched with sweat even in the shade of the gazebo, grateful for Daisy's help so we could finish and head back in to relax inside where there was air conditioning and iced tea in the fridge.

"And...?" I prodded my friend as I ran the tip of my shovel around the inside of the pot and gently tugged the plant free. "What's the gossip?"

Daisy slid one of the hanging pots my way. "Evidently Holt Dupree doesn't drink, doesn't do drugs, doesn't even inhale second-hand smoke, and he's very careful about not being alone with any teenage girls."

Which made complete sense given what the judge has said happened in Louisiana. The guy had an amazing opportunity to make it big. He'd be a fool to screw it up with a scandal or a criminal record.

"And he also went home with Kendra Witt," Daisy confided.

I had no idea who Kendra Witt was, or why my friend thought that was salacious gossip.

"Please tell me she's over the age of eighteen." I patted some extra potting soil around the geranium and shot Daisy a wry glance.

"She's late twenties and unmarried, but her boyfriend took exception to this liaison, and made a whole lot of drunken threats at the party once he realized Kendra had ditched him for the host of the party."

Holt had been sporting a faint bruise on his cheek from the fight with Buck after the concert, but I didn't remember seeing any other injuries. "I take it the boyfriend's buddies restrained him before he could act on those threats?"

Daisy chuckled. "The guy was so blind drunk that he didn't even know his girlfriend and Holt were gone until an hour after they'd left. His friends calmed him down and took him home to sober up."

Sheesh. If the guy was that drunk and inattentive, no wonder his girlfriend took off for greener pastures. I wondered if there would be racy pictures of Kendra forwarded around after today. Hopefully the woman was mature enough to keep any selfies to herself.

"Did you ever hear about a scandal when Holt was in high school involving forwarding inappropriate pictures and texts from a girl?" I asked Daisy.

She frowned for a moment. "You mean Ashley Chen? I didn't know her personally but some of my kids back then used to talk about her. From what I heard she'd been in therapy for clinical depression for a few years. Poor kid vanished after that thing with the pictures and text went down."

"That makes Holt even more of a world class jerk," I commented. "Forwarding things that were meant to be private is bad enough, but to do that to a girl who was known to be troubled is just cruel."

"It is." Daisy moved the newly potted flowers to the ground and grabbed another hanging basket. "The Chen family has big money. They live in that gated community off Cecil Road. The dad holds several pharmaceutical patents, the mom was a socialite with a trust fund— debutante balls and all that. I know it's no excuse, but to a boy from Trenslertown like Holt, a fling with Ashley Chen would have been one heck of a notch on his bedpost."

"Then why forward those pictures and text and ensure that girl will never be anywhere near your bedpost again?" I retorted, plopping another geranium in the empty basket.

Daisy sighed and dusted the loose soil from her hands. "This is going to sound horrible, but to someone who grew up like Holt, girls like Ashley Chen are forever destined to be a one-time, chance thing. What did they have in common? There was no hope for a relationship, even if her parents would have allowed such a thing. There were only bragging rights, the status he'd get for being a poor kid who got a rich-girl in the sack. And he had proof, so he used it."

"How are you defending him?" I demanded, unable to believe that my best friend was sticking up for this jerk. "You counsel troubled teen girls, and you're defending him?"

Daisy raised her hands defensively. "I'm not defending him, just trying to explain the mindset of these kids so you understand where they're coming from when they do these things."

"I don't care how poor he was, that's a horrible thing to do to someone," I sputtered.

"I know, I know. Ashley is probably a really sweet girl and he completely betrayed her trust."

I patted the soil around the geranium with a little more force than necessary. "So you're saying all he cared about was the status he got for one night with a rich girl? How can someone be so selfish, so lacking in any sort of empathy or compassion?"

Daisy handed me the spade and I scooped more dirt into the hanging basket. "Holt is probably only in it for Holt. With a lot of these guys, it doesn't matter who they hurt, or who they step on as long as they get what they want. I'm just trying to tell you that it's often a common mentality for these desperately poor kids. The rich and middle-class kids are 'others' and they believe those rich kids are more than happy to crush them given the chance. They learn to take what they can, claw their way out any way they can, and not lose any sleep over hurting anyone."

I remembered the concert, the girl-next-door with the rusted old car. "Except Violet Smith."

Daisy gave me a sad smile. "Except Violet Smith and those like her, who work themselves to the bone to get two steps ahead. If she'd cheated and stepped on people she would have been six steps ahead with less effort. When poor kids look at Violet as a possible role model, then the local scammer as a possible role model, guess which one they'll pick? The scammer makes more money with less effort. It took Violet years and a whole lot of student loans to get her degree, and now she's got to try to find a job still carrying the stigma of being one of the Smith girls. The drug dealer's got a better life, and all he has to fear is jail—which is where most of these kids think they're going to end up anyway."

I guess incarceration wasn't so much of a threat when most of your family had been in and out of jail your whole life.

44

I put a final pat on the soil and bent to gather up two other hanging baskets. Daisy picked up the other two and gave me a grin.

"Anyway, tell Judge Beck not to worry. Remember the redhead that joined us in the tent after the regatta?"

"Yes, I do." How could I forget? She was beautiful—incredibly sexy in short shorts and a tight tank top. She's walked right up and wrapped her arm around Holt, blatantly marking her territory. Holt hadn't rebuffed her, either.

"That was Kendra Witt, and what Kendra wants, Kendra gets, at least until Holt tells her to shove off."

"Didn't look like he was telling her to shove off," I drawled.

"She's the flavor of the day, or at least of the weekend. She'll be in for a rude awakening Monday, but until then she'll make sure none of the other girls gets too close."

There was one girl who hadn't been the 'flavor of the day'. I remembered the look in Holt's eyes as he'd greeted her, as he'd watched her walk off to her rusted car. "Holt would have never forwarded pictures and texts of Violet Smith," I said, confident that I was speaking the truth.

"No, he wouldn't." Daisy sighed. "Trenslertown kids stick together. That neighbor kid might steal your stuff or get into a fight with you, but when it comes to outsiders, the poor kids stick together like family."

# CHAPTER 7

hat night we hosted a pre-firework barbeque party at our house. Judge Beck had suggested it, partly I think as a sop for Madison not being able to go to the Persimmon Bridge party, and partly to keep the kids all at my house and not off somewhere with Holt Dupree. When the judge had awkwardly asked permission to host the party, I'd warmly told him that this was his home, and that a heads-up was all that was necessary. Besides, I loved Madison and Henry and truly enjoyed when Chelsea and Sean were over, filling up this big old Victorian house like a proper family should.

Coming downstairs into the dining room after my shower, I realized that my house was overfilled—less like a proper family and more like a frat house. I'll give the judge credit, there was not a drop of alcohol in sight, but there were stacks of grilled hamburgers and hot dogs, open chip bags spilling their contents onto the floor, much to Taco's enjoyment, and nearly two dozen bottles of soda. There were also teenagers—lots and lots of teenagers. I looked in the kitchen and out into my yard, and counted, guessing that there were between twelve and fourteen kids here. No, there were another two over by the hot tub. Sixteen.

"Food's on!" Judge Beck shouted as he came in the kitchen door.

I heard the shouts and cheers of the hungry mob, and a stampede of footsteps. Backing into a corner of the dining room so I wouldn't be trampled, I laughed to see the judge make his way through the crowd of noisy, hungry piranhas.

"I'm sorry, this really got out of hand." He ran a hand through his dark blond hair, leaving a streak of charcoal and hamburger grease along his forehead. "They were only supposed to have two friends each, but it spiraled out of control."

"This is small compared to some of the parties Eli and I used to host." I grabbed a napkin off the table, and tried to resist wiping the greasy dark mark from his face. "There were a few times when I was sure the police were going to show up. A dozen hamburger-eating kids won't do anything thirty drunk adults haven't already done."

"I promise we'll clean everything up." He looked around and grimaced. "Although it might need to wait until tomorrow if we're going to make it to the fireworks on time."

"It's fine. Stop worrying."

His brow furrowed. I crunched the napkin in my fist, staring at the streak on his forehead.

"It's just...I saw your face when you came in the kitchen and saw everyone in the back yard—"

"It was probably the same look that you had when carloads of kids started arriving." *Must not wipe his face. Must not wipe his face.*

The judge laughed. "True. I had to ask one of the moms to run out and pick up more burgers and buns. Thankfully she was eager to run an unplanned errand for me. Allison's mom, I think. I can't remember her name."

I'll bet she was helpful. And I'll bet she remembered Judge Beck's name. She probably had it tattooed somewhere on her body. I'd noticed how friendly the single moms had been to my roommate whenever they were dropping their daughters or sons off, and how eager they were with offers of help. Madison had noticed too, and bristled at the sharks circling her father when her parents' divorce wasn't even close to final. I was sure Allison's mom, as well as two or three other moms, would be lingering to chat and flirt tonight after the fireworks when they picked their sons and daughters up to go home. All the while Judge Beck would reply politely, with that bland, clueless smile on his face that said he truly had no idea these women were moving him to the top of their must-date list. And why not? He was a good-looking, fit, successful man in his early forties. Once the divorce was final, he'd have women asking him out right and left. The thought bothered me almost as much as that line of dark grease on his forehead.

Oh, for Pete's sake. I just couldn't stand it anymore. I lifted my napkin, and stood on my tiptoes and met the judge's startled gaze.

"Bend down," I commanded. "You've got grill grease on your forehead."

He obeyed, a bemused expression on his face as I scrubbed at the mark. It didn't want to come off, but rather than send him off to the bathroom, I licked the napkin and kept at it, commanding him to hold still.

By the time I realized what I was doing, the greasy mark was gone, the skin under it somewhat red from my determined efforts. Oh, Lord, I'd just cleaned the judge's face with a saliva-wet napkin, as if he were a child. I held my breath, and my gaze slid from his forehead to meet his own. It was so embarrassing. I wanted to apologize, to say something, anything, but we just stood there, silent, frozen in time, staring into each other's eyes as I still held an upraised, damp, dirty napkin.

He had beautiful eyes. Actually he had beautiful everything. And he was almost twenty years younger than me, not even divorced yet. And I was still aching over the loss of my husband. Was I just as bad as those single mothers who seemed like vultures circling our house? Or worse, because he was far too young for me and I hadn't even been widowed a year yet.

*Idiot. He's forty-two, not twenty-two. You're just lonely and confusing the affection toward friends and newfound family for romantic love.*

Something furry darted past us, breaking the spell— something furry with a hot dog in his mouth….

"Make sure you're covering the food," I called into the other room.

Judge Beck took a step back, laughing as we watched Taco gobble down his stolen treat, then trot back into the kitchen for yet another raid.

"And try not to let the cat out," I added.

\* \* \*

IT WAS another hour before we need to walk the five blocks for the fireworks. I'd always been able to see them from my front porch, but the lower ones and ground displays weren't visible unless you were on the carnival grounds. We would be a mob heading down the sidewalk, but finding parking much closer would have been difficult, and there was no way we could have crammed over a dozen kids into our two vehicles.

I'd grabbed a few blankets to sit on, amused that they'd gotten more use in the last three days than they had in the last decade. I was throwing a few drinks in a soft-sided cooler, when the judge shooed me out, insisting that I go relax while he got everything ready and did a bit of clean up.

I left it all in his hands, scooped up Taco, and headed outside. The cat went into his outdoor cabana-run, and I milled about, picking up a few discarded plates and cups before plopping down in the gazebo to watch the kids. Henry and his friends were playing horseshoes. Madison and her friends were sitting in the grass, checking their cell phones and gossiping. Eli's ghost lurked nearby, then passed through the group of teenage girls to drift beside me as I watched the sun set and eavesdropped.

There was a bit of discussion about a boy that Katie liked, dissecting in minute detail his every word and gesture in an attempt to determine if he reciprocated the girl's interest. Then conversation turned to some vicious slander of Allison's ex-boyfriend in a show of solidarity for how much better off she was without him. Then one of the girls brought up the party at Persimmon Bridge.

I peeked around one of the gazebo posts, sure this would be salt in the wound for Madison. She complained bitterly about how her father wouldn't let her go, and didn't seem any happier when Katie and Allison both chimed in that they'd not been allowed to go either.

"It wouldn't have mattered." Chelsea put an arm around Madison's shoulders. "Once we got there, Holt barely said two words to any of us. He was too busy with that Kendra girl."

"That won't last," Babette scoffed. "Bet he'll be with a different girl tonight."

Maria shrugged. "I don't know. She came up to him at the regatta and I didn't see him trying to dump her."

"Well, she's a fool if she thinks he's going to be with her after he leaves town," Peony announced confidently. "She's just a fling for the holiday."

The other girls agreed, a few of them commenting that Holt was just as much of a player as he'd been in high school —not that any of these girls were old enough to have even known Holt in high school.

"He wasn't always that way," Peony told them. "He dated my sister Violet for two years, and I know he didn't run around on her. Violet doesn't put up with that stuff."

"Yeah, but he dumped her for greener pastures, for the player life," Maria said.

"She dumped him," Peony glared, affronted that Maria would even suggest her sister was the dumpee and not the dumper.

Maria rolled her eyes. "I'm sure that's what she told you. Who in their right mind would ever dump Holt Dupree?"

I tensed, expecting a fight. Peony certainly looked like she was ready to start swinging. Then suddenly, she let out a breath and leaned back against the gazebo. "My stupid sister, that's who dumps Holt Dupree. He loved her. I think he still does. I think if she snapped her fingers, she'd end up with a ring on one of them."

"Doubtful." Maria snorted, and Madison elbowed her in the ribs with a glare.

"It's always the ones that get away they love the most," Madison said. "It's sad. I wonder what he did that she wouldn't forgive him?"

"Did he cheat on her?" Chelsea's voice was full of sympathy. "You said she wouldn't put up with that kind of thing. Maybe he fooled around and she told him to take a hike."

Peony shook her head. "No way. I think Violet is the only girl Holt never cheated on. She said she just didn't like how he'd become, that he wasn't the same boy anymore."

That was greeted with a moment of silence. Then a chorus of 'no' and 'how could that be?' and 'she's crazy'.

Peony shrugged. "Violet wants a boy who just sits back

and lets the world take advantage of him. Not me. I want someone who knows what they want and goes and gets it— someone who isn't afraid to take risks and push his way to the top. Dad always said if people aren't going to get out of your way, then you gotta either push them aside or climb over them."

Madison frowned. "That's mean. There's other ways to get ahead than by screwing over other people."

"Sometimes that's what you have to do," Peony insisted. "Nobody is going to just hand stuff to you on a platter, least not where I grew up. Holt always did what he had to do, and now he's going to make millions and be famous. And Violet could have had all that too, if she hadn't been such a fool and let him go."

I winced, realizing that Peony was just as enthralled with Holt as pretty much every girl in town under the age of thirty. It wasn't surprising. In addition to everything he had going for him, he was someone who'd managed to make it big from her neighborhood. He was a rags-to-riches story. No wonder she admired him over her hardworking and much poorer sister.

They all adored him. And I couldn't wait until the day Holt Dupree left this town and I never had to hear his name again.

## CHAPTER 8

*J*udge Beck and I sat on the blanket alone. The kids had run off to buy smoothies from a nearby vendor with a stern reminder to be back before the show began. It was that solemn moment of first dark, when the dusky notes of twilight had faded from the sky. We had no moonrise yet, the only lights the faint dots of stars and the millions of glowsticks waved about by excited children. It had been ten years since I'd sat on a blanket at the carnival grounds and watched the fireworks. I think Eli and I had even used this same blanket, and probably been in almost the same spot.

Seven months after his accident, he'd been in no condition to make the short trip, even if I could have managed to get him and a wheelchair into the car. Eli's hospital bed in the parlor had been positioned so he could see out the front windows, but the porch overshadowed all but a handful of the colorful bursts of light. Still, I'd sat by Eli's side, watching the ones we could see, and listening to the explosions of the many we couldn't. The whole time I'd assured him that the next year we'd go back down to the carnival grounds to watch. Next year he'd be better, and everything would be back to normal. We'd go to the regatta and the concert and the parade. We'd go to the fireworks.

Next year was the same. The following year I didn't even open the curtains. It just made Eli sad, a reminder of things we'd never have again, experiences we'd never be able to share. Most times he didn't remember anyway, even though as the years went on we tried all sorts of memory devices and note-taking systems to aid him. Worst of all, he knew what he'd lost. He was very aware that events and conversations were slipping like water through his fingers.

"Why don't we go see the fireworks anymore?" he'd fuss at me.

We didn't go because it was so difficult for me to get him in and out of bed, to get the chair through the narrow doorway and down the steps, to get him in the car and the chair in the trunk. I felt bad every time I denied him an outing because it was a struggle for *me*. Sometimes I called Conrad to give me a hand and we'd take Eli out, exhausted by the time we'd gotten him back home and in bed. He'd be angry the whole trip, frustrated that he was helpless to get himself around, unable to remember people's names, or often even where we were going or what we were doing. Half the time he couldn't remember where we'd gone, or confused the excursion with some other place we'd visited or thing we'd done years ago, mashing experiences up like a fruit salad. The outings dwindled to monthly, then twice a year.

He was happier looking at pictures—even of places we'd never been. Pictures brought joy and a scrambled mix of memory and fantasy. Actual outings only brought anger, frustration, and exhaustion.

I still felt terrible that I'd given up, taken the easy way out. Had I just made up excuses for not putting forth the effort? Had I imagined that he was happier not going because it was what *I* wanted? The smart, dry-humored, charming Eli I'd married had died in that accident, but I'd learned to love the sweet, absent-minded man who the accident had left behind. He was short-tempered, often irritated with me and himself, but there were moments where he smiled and held my hand, and I knew he still found joy in life. He mourned the old Eli just as much as I had, but this new Eli often saw beauty in things that the man I'd married hadn't even noticed. Every now and then he'd grasp an old memory from our past, and laugh, and I'd hope the old Eli would be returning as the doctors had at first hoped he might. But it wasn't to be. The old Eli was gone, and these glimpses were no more than ghosts.

No. The ghost in my house was more substantial than these fleeting whispers of the man I'd fallen so deeply in love with when we were college.

And here I sat. With Judge Beck. And as much as I enjoyed having him and his children in my house as my adoptive family, it seemed a betrayal. Eli hadn't been gone for six months, and I was out having fun, doing the things he'd so wanted to do those last ten years. It made me feel guilty. It made me want him here with me, as we'd been all those years ago.

"Miss Kay, I brought you a smoothie."

I looked up into Henry's smiling face. The boy was holding a cup to me, a bendy straw protruding from the plastic lid.

"It's kiwi mango. Is that okay?"

I felt the sting of tears and it took me a second to find my voice. "I love kiwi mango. Thank you so much, Henry."

He grinned and jogged off to sit with his friends on another blanket. Madison and the girls were ten feet away on a blanket of their own—far enough that they had the illusion of independence, but near enough that they were still under Judge Beck's steely eye. I shook off my melancholy and the ghosts of my recent past and hid a smile by sipping my drink. It was the perfect combination of tart and sweet, and an icy cold contrast to the lingering heat of the day.

"The young devil hasn't made an appearance yet," I teased the judge. "Maybe you can relax your vigilance enough to enjoy the evening?"

He grimaced. "It's bad enough being responsible for one teenage girl. What was I thinking to allow Madison to invite an entire posse of them? I'm tempted to put an electric fence around them and stand guard with a shotgun. Their parents would never forgive me if anything improper happened on my watch."

"I'm pretty sure Allison's mom would forgive you just about anything," I teased.

His brow furrowed. "What are you talking about? Is she the one who ran out to get more hamburgers? If anything, I owe *her* one."

"Oh yes you do, and I'm pretty sure she's fantasizing right now about how she's going to collect on that." I gave a few moments for that to sink in. It didn't. Judge Beck was clearly one of those guys who was clueless about the female attention he generated. And I wasn't sure why I felt the need right now to be the one to enlighten him. "In case you didn't notice, all the single moms are eyeing you up, waiting for the divorce to go through so they can pounce."

He blinked in surprise. "I'm not even divorced yet."

"They're waiting, some not so patiently, for that to happen."

He let out a breath and shook his head. "I honestly haven't

even thought that far ahead. I guess I'll eventually want to date again someday. Although it would be terribly awkward for the kids if I dated one of their friends' moms. Imagine if it didn't work out."

"Imagine if it did." I really couldn't stop teasing him on this. It was like I wanted to push him into an uncomfortable conversation. Although, surprisingly, this wasn't as uncomfortable as I'd thought it would be. "Having Allison's mom stay over, and everyone sitting down for breakfast the next morning... Madison would be mortified."

He turned a shocked gaze on me. "*I* would be mortified. That's never going to happen. That sort of thing would only happen when the kids were not with me. In fact, any dating I do would be completely separate from my time with Madison and Henry. I'm not even going to introduce them to anyone unless I'm thinking of marriage. And trust me, I don't believe I'll ever be thinking of marriage again."

It was a passionate speech, and I was now the one shocked. He didn't want to share his family with anyone. Any woman in his life would just be casual, or carefully boxed into the time between family and work. She'd be for adult conversation, and other adult things. She'd be like a mistress on the side, fitting into whatever schedule he had at the moment.

The picture forming in my mind was horrible, and what was worse was that I didn't think the judge realized it. I knew the disintegration of his marriage and this contentious divorce had left scars, but I hadn't realized quite how many.

And far back in the corner of my brain a little voice told me that I was better off as the friend, the roommate, the older widowed lady who'd been allowed into the sanctity of his family, than I would ever be as a romantic interest. The thought was insane. Clearly I was never a romantic interest. I was nearly twenty years his senior. We had nothing in common. We weren't even attracted to each other.

*You're attracted to him*, the little voice told me. Well, of course I was. Duh. As if any woman with eyes wouldn't be. Unbidden memories rose of us at my dining room table, files spread everywhere, dishes with the remains of dinner pushed aside. There was an easy comradery between us. We'd bonded when I'd been researching the history of my sideboard, and he'd been just as interested and enthusiastic on solving the mystery of its former owners as I had. But comradery didn't equate to romance. And I was older. And recently widowed. And he not even divorced and still wounded and bitter.

"How about you?" The resolute, somewhat harsh expression on his face had shifted to one of mischief. I swear, dark as it was, I saw his eyes twinkle.

"Me what?" I firmly put all the stupid thoughts of romance away. No doubt it had been those movies I'd been watching lately. No more Hallmark Channel for me. Documentaries from this point forward. Or old sitcoms.

"Dating?" He laughed as he saw my expression. "If you're going to grill me about my plans for future romantic encounters, then it's only fair I question you."

Where in the world *would* I meet potential romantic interests? My job as a skip tracer at an investigative and bail bonds company didn't provide many opportunities to meet eligible men my age. Our clients were either facing jail time, or hiring us to dig up dirt on a cheating wife. The police detectives and officers that came in and out of our office all appeared to be in their twenties. Was there an online dating site for women my age? Singles meet-ups? The very thought was exhausting.

"Well, I've been going to the nursing home weekly to visit

with Matt's father. Maybe I'll find some hot widower there on fried chicken day."

He laughed. "Kay, you're not *that* old."

"It's the perfect place to meet men," I insisted, trying in vain to keep from laughing myself. "Everyone there already teases me about being Maurice's girlfriend."

"They probably think you're Matt's girlfriend." He shifted closer on the blanket and jostled my arm with his elbow. "You should date Matt."

The words felt like a blow to my middle. Matt was a good-looking guy, my age, long-divorced and stable. He was fun. I met him weekly to have lunch with his dad at the nursing home. I'd invited him to my neighborhood barbeque. He was a social guy, very active in community service projects and charities. He golfed with Judge Beck on occasion. He and I were friends and I'd finally gotten through to him that there wouldn't be anything more between us. The girls and I were even going to the Fourth of July Bingo Fundraiser tonight that he'd organized at the VFW. I wasn't going to date Matt. I didn't want to date Matt.

"No, I'm not ready. I buried my husband less than six months ago. I'm not ready for that." It came out more raw that I'd intended, and the expression on Judge Beck's face changed like lightning. He reached out and gripped my hand.

"I'm sorry, Kay. I forget how soon it's been. Please forgive me. I never should have suggested it."

"It's okay. I know I don't always act like the grieving widow." I didn't. And when I caught myself having a good time, not thinking about Eli, the guilt roared in along with the grief. But the grief now came in degrees, not the overwhelming tsunami it had been that first month. Sometimes the grief was a flood, and sometimes a gentle tide flowing in to shore then ebbing softly away, leaving guilt in its wake—guilt because it was far too soon for me to have a lessening of grief. It hadn't even been six months yet. It should still be a tsunami, and every time it wasn't I felt like perhaps I hadn't loved Eli as much as I claimed.

If I'd loved him I would still be paralyzed with the pain of his loss. If I'd loved him I would have made the effort every year to get him out to go see the fireworks. If I'd loved him, I would have noticed the signs of his stroke in time to get help and save his life. If I'd loved him, I wouldn't be sitting here enjoying the way Judge Beck's hand felt wrapped around mine.

"If you acted like the grieving widow twenty-four-seven, then I'd be really worried." He squeezed my hand reassuringly. "When my uncle died, my aunt went to Europe for three weeks to help herself cope. His death was devastating for her, and she needed distance and distraction to help her process it, or I think she would have gone crazy. Let your heart ache and heal the way it needs to."

The first test firework shot into the sky, an explosion of thin white sparks that lit and vanished in a blink. Light, and then darkness once more.

"Kay, don't begrudge yourself moments of joy. Don't blame yourself for seeing the beauty in a sunset, or sharing laughter with friends, or feeling affection, even the stirrings of love, for another. I didn't know Eli, but from what you'd told me, he wouldn't want you to live the rest of your life in tears."

*"I'm not going to get better, am I?" Eli's voice had been monotone. He'd stared at the wall. It had been as if he were reciting IRS tax code. We'd just watched the last firework fade from the sky from the window of the parlor that had become my husband's bedroom, his hand in mine.*

*"You get better every day. Every day," I had insisted. He did. It was just that those improvements had been miniscule, and often countered by lost ground in other areas.*

*"Never better." My eyes had widened as Eli's voice rose with emotion. "My life, all it will be is notes to remember. Recordings to remember. Waking up and not knowing. Too much. Too much and not enough time."*

*Tears stung my eyes. He'd been frustrated, angry. Still, that anger and frustration had been so much better than the years of apathy that had followed.*

*"Will I be a doctor again? Work again? Ever?"*

*I'd sworn to always be honest with him, but if I had answered 'no', would I have been taking away the only thing that kept him trying, kept him moving forward? So instead I'd replied: "I don't know."*

*He'd turned to me, his face once again impassive, gaze distant. "You will leave me."*

*I shivered with sudden cold at the memory of his words. It wasn't that I hadn't thought about it. I'd feared that I would spend the rest of my life caring for him—a man that most of the time I didn't recognize. Was it wrong if there were fleeting moments where I wanted out, fleeting moments where I thought of putting him in a care facility and trying to go on with my life? He hadn't been the only one who'd lost everything in that accident. It had all felt so terribly unfair.*

*Poor me. Poor little me.*

*"No. I won't leave you." I'd reached out and smoothed his hair, receiving no reaction at all from him. "For better or for worse. In sickness and in health. I vowed before God, Eli, and I won't break that promise."*

*His gaze had focused, and for a brief moment I'd glimpsed the man I'd said those vows to at the altar. "Well, you should. You should leave me. You don't deserve this...burden."*

No, Eli wouldn't have wanted me to spend the rest of my life in tears, eaten away by sorrow. He would have wanted me to catch my breath at a beautiful sunset, to go to late-night bingo with my friends, to laugh...and love. Eventually love. When I was ready.

A dozen fireworks shot into the sky, colors spreading like streaks of spilled paint as the crowd cheered. The red, green, and white twinkled then vanished, a skeleton of gold dust remaining briefly in the sky before the next round hid it from view. I made the appropriate 'ooo' noise, and lost myself in the beauty of it all, aware that throughout it all, Judge Beck made no move to let go of my hand.

# CHAPTER 9

"*W*ait, did he say B12?" Kat waved her stamper frantically scanning her six cards. I'd abandoned Judge Beck with his hoard of teenagers and gone out with my girlfriends to the late-night bingo at the VFW. It was from ten until midnight—far later than most of our bedtimes. If they hadn't been serving coffee, I would have been face-down on my bingo sheets.

"G46."

"No! Slow down I haven't finished looking for B12 yet." Kat made a T with her hands. "Time out. I'm calling time-out."

"There are no time-outs in Bingo, girl." Olive chuckled.

"Here. Stamp here." Daisy pointed to one of Kat's cards only to have Suzette slap her hand away.

"No helping. I'm gonna win this Bakery Madness basket. It's mine, mine, mine. Come on N35. Come on." Suzette clasped her hands together as if in prayer.

"You gonna share that Bakery Madness basket?" Olive asked, grinning.

"Everything but the sand tarts. I love me some sand tarts.

My grandmother used to make them so thin that they made an audible 'snap' when you bit into them. With a little, blanched, half almond in the middle. Mmm."

Sand tarts. They weren't actually tarts, but cookies, like ginger snaps only buttery with a hint of an almond and vanilla flavor. I had an old recipe for those somewhere. If I could find it, I'd make a batch for Suzette.

Or she could just win the basket.

"Was that G46 or G56?" Kat lifted a hand to run through her hair. Unfortunately, that hand had the stamper and she now had a streak of red in her dark curls. "I don't want to screw up because if I yell 'bingo', and I read off my card and I've got something wrong, the scorn of every man and woman in this VFW hall will be on my head."

"Did someone say 'bingo'?" The announcer asked.

Kat's eyes widened, and her lips clamped shut. It was suddenly so quiet in the VFW that I swear I heard a gnat fly by.

"N36," the announcer continued.

"Oh, *come on!*" Suzette threw her hands heavenward.

"Bingo," Olive announced.

Suzette shot her a narrowed glance that made Olive laugh. "Oh, don't worry honey. Those sand tarts are all yours."

"Yes!" Suzette did a fist pump, then listened intently as Olive read off her card.

"How is that a win?" she demanded.

"Inside corners," Olive told her. "There's seven patterns to win, unless it's a Blackout game, then you have to fill your whole card."

"Dang," Kat muttered looking down at her cards. "I was so close. One more and I would have had that basket."

"Me too." Daisy practically had a table all to herself with dozen cards around her.

"Well, not me." I waved at my cards with their scattered stamp marks. "Lady Luck is not my friend tonight."

"Next time," Daisy promised me. Then we all fell silent as Matt delivered the Bakery Madness basket to Olive as if he were presenting Excalibur to King Arthur. We all regarded the basket with an admiring moment of silence, then tore into it like a pack of starving wolves. Olive handed over the sand tarts to Suzette with a warm smile. I got the chocolate peanut butter no-bake cookies, and bit into one, feeling the sugar race through my veins. Between these and the coffee I'd probably be up all night, which meant I'd be exhausted at work tomorrow. The prospect was kind of exciting, like a return to my youth when bleary-eyed mornings were the norm. I hadn't stayed up late partying in a long time, and those parties of my youth hadn't been in a VFW bingo hall, fueled by coffee and baked goods.

"Here. You need to try one of these." I handed a no-bake cookie to Matt. After his solemn delivery he'd begun selling cards for the next round.

"Thanks." He grinned and popped it in his mouth, waving the cards at me as he chewed.

"Six," I told him, handing him a ten. In spite of this being the Fourth of July and after the fireworks, the hall was packed. I hoped he was making his goal for the Serenity Park Playground Equipment Fund.

"Mrf," he replied, exchanging the cards for my cash. Many women, including Daisy, carefully selected which cards they wanted. I, on the other hand, preferred to let fate do the work for me. So far this evening, fate was being uncooperative. I hadn't won a thing.

An elderly lady in a wheelchair with two helpers won the Choco-love Basket, much to Kat's dismay. Daisy finally scored with the Popcorn-and-a-Movie basket, and I won the last basket of the evening—Gaming-Fun. It included an old-fashioned Parcheesi set, a deck of Uno cards, and Yahtzee. It also included a bag of gummy bears that we quickly devoured.

It was midnight. People were starting to file out of the hall, happily content with their winnings, or optimistic that next time they'd be the lucky ones. This had been fun. Matt organized these monthly, each night benefiting a different local charity. I really wanted to make this a regular thing for me and my friends, and maybe give Matt a hand in soliciting for the gift baskets. He'd been hard at work all night, but clearly enjoying himself just as much as those of us who were happily stamping their cards. I honestly didn't know when the guy slept between all his volunteer work and visiting his father. I got tired just watching him sometimes.

But not tonight. I was wide awake tonight. And it was midnight.

"Who wants to go to Mick's?" Olive asked.

Olive, the woman who had to put on a suit and go to an accounting job in about six hours, wanted to go to a bar.

"I do! I do!" Suzette waved her hand in the air and laughed. She was flushed and giddy. I'd never seen her so happy. It made me wonder what had been in those sand tarts.

"I'm game," Daisy announced. Kat didn't take much convincing, and I decided I might as well join them. It wasn't like I'd be able to go to sleep for another three or four hours anyway with all the coffee I'd been drinking.

I went over to say goodbye to Matt, and tell him how much fun I'd had this evening. He was packing away bingo supplies, talking cheerfully with the announcer.

"We raised over eight hundred by my estimate," he told me. "That's sixteen hundred with the matching funds from Sentry Bank and Trust."

I knew from previous conversations that sixteen hundred wouldn't buy a lot in the way of playground equipment, but it all added up. Matt was the very embodiment of patience, chipping away at his charity goals slowly and steadily.

"Well, I had a wonderful time and I think you have a new bingo convert in Suzette. She'll be here every month as long as you've got a bakery basket as a prize."

He laughed. "It's from Patents in Milford. Tell her they donate one each month."

"She'll be happy to hear it." I motioned toward the door. "We're heading over to Mick's. Do you want to join us when you're done here? We'll probably be sipping seltzer water and coming down off of our caffeine and sugar high until they close."

He wiggled his eyebrows. "The only guy surrounded by five gorgeous women? I wish I could, but this is going to take a while, and I want to get all the accounting and reports done tonight, too. Next month I'll make Rich do it for me and join you ladies."

"I don't know if I can do this sort of thing every month," I laughed. "We old gals are usually in bed by ten, not out playing bingo and shutting down the local pub."

"This month is the only Moonlight Bingo. Usually we start at six and finish up at nine. Next month we could grab a nightcap after and still have you to bed before midnight."

"When I turn into a pumpkin." I smiled. "Next time, then."

As I turned to leave, I heard him call after me.

"Next time." And then, "Kay? Be careful driving home, okay? It's the Fourth, and late. Might be some drunks on the road tonight."

# CHAPTER 10

*W*e were all rowdy and riding a sugar high from a combination of the contents of the Bakery Madness Basket and my gummy bears as we took over Mick's Bar and Grill. Each of us nursed a bottle of domestic beer and played the most horrendous dart games ever.

We shut the place down. At two o'clock in the morning I stood in the parking lot, waving goodbye to my friends and climbing into my car. I felt like I was in my twenties again, partying it up until the wee hours at a bar. The only difference was that I was stone sober after only having one beer all night, and I was coming off of a sugar high. And my back was killing me from those horrible chairs at bingo. I didn't remember my back hurting from chairs when I was twenty. I could sit on boulders for hours, sleep crooked in the passenger seat of a car, or camp out with only my rucksack for a pillow and wake up refreshed and ready to go. Now I slept on my high-quality mattress with my ergonomic pillow and often woke up feeling like I'd spent the night on the floor.

In spite of it being July, I turned the seat heater on in my car to try to help relieve my back, and headed home. A few blocks from the bar I was regretting my late night impulse. The sugar was wearing off and I felt exhausted. Taking the back roads would shave ten minutes off my trip, and right now ten minutes closer to my bed sounded amazing.

There was only one problem. The shortcut took me down a familiar road, one that had me gripping the steering wheel with white-knuckled hands at the thought. I hadn't been down this road in ten years. This was the road Eli always took to get to the hospital faster, or to get home to me faster. He'd traveled it in the pre-dawn hours, or after sunset, or even in the middle of the day when his overnight shift at the hospital spilled far past the morning.

Memories flooded me of *that* morning. I remembered the feel of the mattress shifting as he got up in the dark, the soft noise of dresser drawers and clothing being put on, the kiss he gave me before he left.

"Love you. See you soon," he'd said. And then I felt his lips on my temple, felt the brush of his smooth, freshly shaven skin, smelled his aftershave.

"When?" I had mumbled, trying to remember his schedule for the week.

"Late tonight if everything goes well. Tomorrow morning if it doesn't. Don't expect me for dinner."

I always hated his surgeon's hours, and for a brief second I'd lain there in bed resenting his job, wishing that he was home more. But Eli's work was his passion, and I knew he wouldn't be happy doing anything else. I'd heard the 'snick' of the door closing, heard the faint noise of his car starting up, then had gone back to sleep. The phone call had woken me.

Driving to the hospital with my heart in my throat, I'd realized that I hadn't replied to Eli that morning, hadn't told him that I loved him too. Yes, he knew it, but I was so afraid that I'd never get the chance to say that to him again, so afraid of what the doctors weren't telling me over the phone.

That morning I'd taken the short cut, driven past the scene of the accident and nearly had to pull off the road. Somehow I'd forced down the panic attack at the broken trees, torn-up dirt, glass and metal still all over the asphalt. I never went back. It had been ten years since I'd been down that road.

Ten years. It was time for me to face the past, stare down my fear, and take the short cut.

It was dark on that unlit country road—two lanes with barely enough along the side to be called a shoulder. Steep banks and ditches were on the other sides of that poor excuse for a shoulder, and beyond that nothing but trees. I knew there were houses back there somewhere, that farms lay beyond those woods, but as I made my way down the road, it seemed as if I were the only soul for miles.

Well, me and a pickup truck that came up from behind and passed at a speed I would never have attempted on this road. I remembered Matt's comments about drunks, and hoped that whoever it was in the truck made it home safely.

Rounding the curve where Route 2 intersected Jones Road, I saw the backend of the pickup swing out, then jerk suddenly into the other lane. Headlights lit the road from the opposite direction, and the driver ahead of me overcorrected and lost control. There was a blinding flash of light as the oncoming car came around the corner. The pickup skidded, rocking wildly as it careened back into my lane. I slammed on the brakes, steering through the antilock controls, blinded by the sudden difference in the dark overcast night and the headlights boring into my eyes.

I couldn't see. There was a crunch, the shriek of rubber on pavement. The seatbelt locked, holding me in place. I blinked, my hands tightly gripping the wheel as I took a much-needed breath. My car was stopped in my lane. I didn't have a deflated airbag in my face, so I must not have hit anything. Looking around I saw the oncoming car in a ditch, headlights pointing past me down the road. The pickup was nowhere to be seen.

That jerk in the pickup had caused an accident and fled the scene. My blood boiled at the thought.

With a shaking hand, I put my car in park and opened my door, making my way over to the car in the ditch. I could see the airbag had inflated. Before I'd even crossed the median, I had my cell phone out and dialed 911.

"I need an ambulance at Jones Road just east of Route 2. There's a car that's been in an accident with a hit-and-run. I don't know how badly the driver is injured, or if there are any passengers."

It was amazing how calm and detailed I could be when my brain was scrambled and my emotions were going into overdrive. There was some part of me that took control, and of that I was grateful because the other part of my brain kept seeing another car, mangled beyond recognition in a police impound lot where they'd towed it, and Eli in a hospital bed with tubes and monitors beeping and making horrible rhythmic suction noises.

I heard the dispatch operator talking in the background, the super-speed typing as well as her assurance that she was on the phone with me, ready to guide me through any emergency medical attention I needed to provide.

I didn't want to do this. I wanted to get in my car and drive away far from all the horrible memories this was bringing back. But someone had stopped for Eli, and that had made all the difference in the world. It meant my husband had continued to live for ten additional years. He might have not been the same man he'd been before. He might not have always been happy that he'd not died at the scene of that accident. He might have been frustrated with the hand that God had dealt him, but he'd lived.

I would be forever grateful to that unnamed person who'd called in the accident, who'd shouted their panic into the phone about the blood and the man wedged tight in his mangled car. Who'd waited by his side until the ambulance arrived. If Eli had died there by the side of the road, I would have wanted there to be another person nearby, just in case he'd opened his eyes and needed that reassurance that someone cared while he breathed his last.

I got to the car door and nearly fainted in relief when it easily opened.

"Are you okay?"

The man in the driver's seat turned a wide-eyed expression my way and nodded. His face was red and splotchy. I wasn't sure what was from the airbag and from any more serious injury.

"I called for an ambulance. They'll be here soon. Where do you hurt?"

The woman from 911 was like a bee buzzing in my ear, asking me to check this and check that, but everything seemed to be moving in slow motion. I didn't want to grab this guy and yank him out of the car or paw him when I didn't know what kind of injuries he might have suffered.

"Chest hurts," he gasped. "And my face. Think I might have broke my nose."

'Chest hurts' was what worried me the most. "Can you get out of the car? If I release your seatbelt, do you think you can get out?"

The woman in my ear was saying something about checking his pulse and keeping him calm and still because of shock or something. I had no idea. She was like background noise as I looked into this man's dark brown eyes and wondered if he had a wife waiting at home for him, or kids expecting pancakes for breakfast.

I unbuckled the seatbelt and put my arm into the car for the man to grasp. He was strong and not exactly a light-weight but I was able to get him out of the vehicle. Somehow I managed and the man stood, leaning against the side of his car, breathing heavily.

"I swerved to avoid that truck," he told me. "Managed not to hit him head on, but we scraped pretty bad along the driver's side."

"It wasn't your fault. I was behind him and he swerved over the center line. It was a blind corner and he was in your lane. He was totally in the wrong, and the jerk left the scene."

"Probably drunk," the man told me. He swayed and I grabbed his shoulders, easing him down the side of his car so he sat on the grass.

"How is your chest feeling now? Keep talking to me. I need you to keep talking to me."

"Better." The man took a careful breath and looked down the road in the direction he'd come from. I was beginning to hear the faint sound of sirens, growing louder as they neared. The shrill noise cut off abruptly as a beam of headlights came around the corner. The narrow illumination brought the heavily wooded shoulders into soft focus, and I saw crushed saplings, trees with fresh scars gleaming white against their brown bark. A shadow darkened a patch of briars even in the lights of the oncoming vehicle. I shivered, knowing how many accidents this sharp corner had seen over the decades, how many fatalities this stretch of road had chalked up. It seemed a car or truck lost control on this curve every few months, and once every year or so, someone lost their life here. Just last fall a dump truck had rolled over right where the injured trees stood. The driver had lived, but they'd needed to call in a helicopter to rush him to the trauma center.

This man seemed to have been lucky. Many weren't. Eli hadn't been. It had been before dawn when he was on his way to prep for an early surgery. An icy road. An oncoming truck crossing the center line. I closed my eyes and envisioned what I supposed had happened based on what I'd seen of our car and read in the police report. The truck had clipped our sedan, sending it into a spin into the woods where it had rolled over several times, slamming the driver's side into a tree. It had taken paramedics half an hour to free Eli from the twisted metal.

When I opened my eyes, I saw the ghost. "Eli?" I whispered, taking a step forward. The shadowy figures I saw were visually almost identical, but I knew right away this one wasn't Eli. I swallowed hard, wondering which of the many people who had lost their lives on this road this was, then turned back to the injured man.

The fire department arrived on the scene, and I stood apart as they spoke to the man, shining a light in his eyes and asking him questions. I knew these guys. They were volunteers, and I'd seen them often enough at their annual donation drive and various fundraisers.

A police car pulled up, and again I saw the shadowy figure in the beam of the headlights. The light illuminated the woods, and I frowned. The scarred trees were too raw, their injuries too recent to have been from that dump truck rollover. Locust Point was a small town, and this road close to our city limits. Any accident that caused this much damage wouldn't have gone unreported.

And that shadow...it didn't feel like Eli or that elderly woman who had died two years ago. This was a man. Young. Angry. Furious that his life had been cut short just when everything he'd ever wanted had been in his hands.

I hadn't seen the pickup truck drive off. Yes, there was a curve in the road, but I'd been blinded by headlights and distracted, trying to avoid the accident taking place right before me. I'd watched the pickup veer across the center line, then overcorrect. I'd slammed on my brakes, seen the oncoming car swerve then careen toward the ditch on the side of the road. I'd heard a crash, the sound of metal against metal, against wood, of brush mowed down. I hadn't seen anything else. I hadn't seen the truck that had been in front of me actually negotiate the curve.

Could it….? My heart pounded in my chest as I walked past the sheriff's deputy climbing out of his car. Feeling numb, I pulled my cell phone back out of my pocket and turned on the flashlight app. There were no skid marks in the road beyond the ones belonging to the car in the ditch. There was nothing beyond the churned-up dirt, the flattened bushes, the gashes in the tree trunks to indicate someone had failed to navigate the turn. I turned my light down the embankment and into the woods, again noticing the dark shadowy figure. Slowly I made my way past the ghost to perch at the edge of the road, looking through the broken woods.

There, hidden by the trees, the brush, the slope of the embankment, and the moonless night was the pickup truck that had been in front of me. It was a twisted chunk of metal and broken glass, covered in mud and broken branches as it lay on its side.

I immediately remembered our sedan in the impound lot, still muddy, the upholstery, the dashboard, and the windshield still stained with blood. So many nights I'd envisioned Eli's accident as if I'd been on the side of the road watching it, or as if I'd been in the passenger seat. Right now, I was doing the same thing with this truck.

"Guys?" I croaked out. "Officer?"

Nothing could make me go down there. Nothing. I didn't want to see it. It had taken me nearly a decade to get over the nightmares after Eli's accident. I couldn't go through that again.

"Officer!" Somehow I managed to find my voice and shout. "The truck that was in front of me is down here. It's... it's bad."

I heard them radioing in for additional help, felt someone push past me and skid down the hill, sliding partway down on his hip. The deputy yanked on the mangled door, grabbing the flashlight off his utility belt and adding that much stronger beam to the one from my cell phone.

The shadow edged up next to me and I shivered, folding my arms across my chest. From the rush of paramedics scrambling down to the truck, the crack of them wrenching the door off with their equipment, I assumed that someone in there had a chance. The ghost hovered near my shoulder telling me otherwise. Either there were two people, or more, in the truck or the first responders yanking the door off were fighting a battle they'd already lost.

They gently eased someone from the passenger seat onto a board then there was a flurry of activity. I caught myself on the edge of hyperventilation and edged back onto the road where I couldn't see what was happening down the embankment.

The other man was sitting in the opening of the ambulance, a blood pressure cuff on his arm. He looked better. He looked like he was fine, but I wasn't sure if my perception was off because of what I was imagining in the other vehicle.

Another ambulance arrived. The paramedics brought a girl up on the stretcher. She had blood on her face and hair and what I could see of her clothing. I recognized her, even with the blood. Peony Smith. No, it couldn't be Peony Smith, not at two o'clock in the morning. Peony Smith was only fifteen years old. No, it had to be her older sister, Violet.

Suddenly it was hard for me to breathe. Violet. The smart girl who had struggled to pull herself out of poverty, who'd managed to get her degree with need-based scholarships, loans, and whatever jobs she could find. I hoped she was okay. I hoped more than anything that a girl who'd done all the right things didn't die at twenty-two, or end up like Eli. Life couldn't be that cruel to do that to a young girl, even if they'd done it to a middle-aged doctor.

They loaded her into the ambulance and I turned to see the other stretcher come up, this one with a zippered body bag.

The deputy approached me, notepad out, ready for my statement. I gave him a shaky smile, recognizing Miles Pickford from the times he'd been in to see J.T.

"Sorry Kay. I didn't mean for you to wait this long, or…" he grimaced. "Or for you to see that. That girl owes her life to you, though. She's gonna make it and that's because you saw that truck down there."

"Is it Violet Smith?" My gaze was drawn to the ambulance once again.

"I don't know, she's unconscious. Did you recognize her? I'm sure her purse and ID are somewhere in the truck." Miles gave me a sympathetic pat on my shoulder. I'd always liked him, young and enthusiastic with his buzz-cut hair, broad shoulders, and kind brown eyes.

"Do you need to sit down?" He steered me to the passenger seat of his car, swinging the door open and taking my elbow as I sank onto the cushion.

"Thanks." I leaned against the seat back, collecting my thoughts for a moment. "I was driving back from Mick's— we'd gone there after bingo at the VFW. The truck passed me about a quarter mile back and when I came around the first turn, I saw it swerve into the other lane."

"Drunk?"

"I don't know." I closed my eyes to remember exactly what happened. "No, he wasn't drifting over the line like he was drunk or falling asleep. It was like he'd lost control of the car, like someone was trying to grab the wheel from him, or he was on icy pavement, or something happened to his steering."

"Probably drunk and the girl tried to grab the wheel when he drifted into the other lane," Miles commented as he wrote.

I went to protest, but decided against it. He'd probably seen far more accidents, and far more drunk drivers, than I had. Maybe I was wrong.

"Either way, when the oncoming car came around the turn, he was still in the wrong lane. These curves are really sharp, and with the trees it's hard to see the lights from an oncoming car until they're almost around the corner."

"Mmm hmm," he mumbled. "Didn't look like a head-on though."

"No. Both vehicles swerved and I was blinded by the headlights, but I heard a crash and once I got stopped and looked, I saw the car in the ditch. I didn't see the truck anywhere, so I thought they made the turn and kept going—a hit-and-run." I shook my head. "If I hadn't been looking in that direction when the lights of your cruiser came around the corner and noticed the fresh damage on the trees…"

"Mr. Coleman told us he thought it was a hit-and-run as well."

It wasn't. "I hate this road," I told Miles, my voice wavering. "I hate it."

"Me too, Kay." He finished his notes and stuffed the pad into his back pocket. "I wish they'd widen it, or buy up a bunch of this land and straighten it out. Too many accidents happen here."

I shivered, thinking of Eli, of whoever had been in the truck with Violet Smith. Looking over at the black body bag, I saw a shadowy figure hovering next to it. The ambulance was just pulling away with the girl, another was arriving to take away the other occupant of the truck—the one who hadn't been so lucky.

One night, and two lives changed forever. Three lives changed, because I was never ever going to drive this road again. Never.

## CHAPTER 11

*I*t was close to four in the morning when I got home. The first thing I did was sit in the driveway and call in sick to work. It wasn't just that I'd be going in on three hours' sleep, I truly couldn't manage to deal with skip traces and bail bond requests right now. I wasn't in any state of mind to do research or write reports. Maybe I should have gone. Maybe it would have helped me snap out of the panic and horror if I'd gotten a shower and headed in as if nothing had happened, but I couldn't. All I wanted to do was curl up on the couch with Taco and a blanket and sleep it all away.

Well aware that everyone else in my house was sound asleep, I carefully opened the door and tiptoed across the creaky wooden floors.

*The soft sounds of drawers opening and closing, the rustle of clothes being put on, the quiet creak of socked feet on the old floors. "Love you. See you soon."*

I wrapped my arms around my chest and bent at the middle, squeezing hard to push the pain away and keep myself from collapsing to the floor. Taco broke the spell, trotting up with a sharp 'meow', and rising to brush himself against my leg. I bent down to pick him up, and he pushed his head into my hands, purring loudly.

"Someone died tonight," I told the cat. "Someone died ten years ago, too." I buried my face in his fur. "A part of me died, that morning ten years ago, and I think that me is gone forever."

*I left my car in the ambulance bay with the keys on the seat, too hurried to search for a parking spot, not caring if they towed it. I ran through the front lobby, down the halls, taking the stairs because I couldn't wait for the elevator. Tears blurred everything into a soft watercolor of white and beige and I choked back sobs as I raced past the nurses at the ICU desk. Their eyes followed, but they didn't stop me because they knew—they knew that I had to hurry before it was too late.*

*I love you. Don't leave me; I love you.*

Taco rumbled against my chest, my fingers deep in the soft fur, stoking and accepting what comfort he could give. I couldn't go to bed, not with all these memories bubbling to the surface. Bed is where I'd seen him last before the accident. It's where I'd been when I'd gotten the call. It's where we'd laid side-by-side in sleep, not bothering to make love that night because we were tired and Eli had to get up early and we had the rest of our lives to make love to each other. *Love you. See you soon.*

Instead of the bed, I sat on the couch and cried until Taco's fur was wet with my tears, until a hint of gray tinged the dark sky. Then I got up and put some quiet music on Henry's entertainment console, wrapped myself in a huge blanket, and fell asleep on the couch with Taco purring in my arms.

\* \* \*

THEY WERE WHISPERING. *They were whispering because they didn't* want me to hear. But I didn't need to hear what they were saying because I knew. The body in the bed didn't even look like Eli. There were monitors and tubes. They'd made an effort to straighten his limbs, but were obviously holding off on surgery until he was stable.

He wasn't stable. And from the whispers I knew they were expecting the shriek of those monitors any minute. Grief slid over me, oily and fetid, then something lit like a spark in my chest. This couldn't happen—not to Eli and not to me. We were too young. We were good people. He'd had a patient prepped for surgery this morning. What had happened to his patient? Eli would be so distressed that his patient would be waiting. He never kept his patients waiting, said it was rude and disrespectful, that their time was just as important as his and if he couldn't manage his schedule then he was a poor excuse for a doctor.

"What happened to Mr. Locke?" I asked the whispering voices.

There was shocked silence.

"Mr. Locke," I insisted. "What happened? Eli will want to know about his patient."

"Rescheduled...another doctor...possibly next Thursday..."

I let out a relieved breath that Mr. Locke wasn't still sitting in a room, waiting for my husband to arrive. Then it sunk in that it would be a long time before Eli could wield a scalpel again.

What was I thinking? He was going to die. They'd cut most of his clothing off, but there was still blood dried on his skin, barely visible among the millions of cuts from a shattered windshield and huge red marks that would be purple and green bruises if he lived long enough. I looked past the damaged skin, past the hoses and monitors and saw the twisted angles of his body. I felt so helpless, so damned helpless. Why was this happening to us? We were good people. Why was this happening to us?

Awareness swam to the surface. The whispers were in a child's voice. Dreams slid away like fog in the morning sun and I blinked open my eyes to see Henry and Madison looking down at me in confusion.

"Is my bed-head that horrible?" I tried to joke.

"Couldn't you sleep?" Henry asked. "Sometimes Mom sleeps on the couch when she can't fall asleep in her bed."

"Coffee or cocoa?" Madison twisted her hands in front of her chest, as if she didn't know what to make of my spending the night on the couch.

I pushed the blanket aside and swung my feet off the couch, sitting up. Sometime in the night Taco had abandoned me. He was probably in the kitchen standing impatiently by his food dish. "Neither, but thank you for the offer, Madison. I think I'm just going to go upstairs to bed. I'm not going in to work today."

Henry frowned. "Are you sick? Can we get you something? Chicken soup?"

Blech. Not at seven in the morning.

"No thanks, Henry." I left the kids without any further explanation and climbed up the stairs to my room. My steps quickened as I heard water splashing in the bathroom. I didn't want to explain to the children, and I didn't want to explain to Judge Beck either. It was all still so raw.

I changed out of my crumpled clothing from the night before, sliding into soft pajamas and brushing my teeth before climbing into bed. I hoped Taco didn't mind getting breakfast a few hours late this morning. Maybe the kids would feed him for me.

I'd laid there, sleep elusive as I stared bleary-eyed at the ceiling for what felt like an hour when there was a soft knock at my door.

"Kay? Are you all right? Can I come in?"

It seemed there was no escaping Judge Beck. The kids must have told him. I didn't have the heart to turn him away and have him worrying about me all day, so I told him to come in, realizing too late how strange it was to have him in my bedroom.

He must have felt the same because he stopped three steps in with a weird, embarrassed expression on his face. "I'm sorry, I didn't mean to...the kids said you were sick? That you slept downstairs last night?" He looked at a spot above my head. "I'm hoping you just had a bit too much fun with your friends last night and aren't actually sick."

He thought I might be hungover. I smiled, remembering my one beer, then the smile faded as I remembered everything else.

"I didn't get home until four. There was an accident, and I needed to stay and wait for the ambulance and to file a police report."

His gaze dropped to my face and in three strides he was sitting on the edge of my bed. "My God, are you okay? Are you hurt? How's your car? What happened?"

"I'm fine. I witnessed the accident. A guy passed me and clipped an oncoming car." I tried for a convincing smile. "I was too tired to go in today. I'll be okay once I get some sleep."

His eyebrows went up. "If you're here in bed and not guzzling a pot of coffee and heading in to work, then it must have been a pretty terrible accident."

I felt a knot loosen in my chest and the words spill from me as I told him about the injured man, about how I almost hadn't seen the other vehicle that had gone off the road just at the sharpest point in the curve in the road.

"I didn't see the driver, but the girl was young." I shuddered. "I think it might have been Violet Smith, one of Peony's older sisters. It looked like her, but it was dark, and there was blood. Oh no. Madison. Her friend's sister."

Judge Beck took a deep breath and let it out in a whoosh.

"I won't say anything to Madison until we know who the girl was. And the driver as well. A boy, you said?"

"I'm sure the deputy referred to the driver as a 'he'. They didn't tell me names or anything. Probably because the one was unconscious and the other dead and they'd need to find ID and notify the next of kin." A chill ran through me once more. The broken trees, the torn-up dirt on the shoulder. There would be bits of metal, shards of glass in the road that the police couldn't sweep away. *Love you. See you soon.*

The judge reached out to pat my shoulder, his hand warm and strong and reassuring. "What can I do for you? Do you want me to call and get the names of the accident victims? Find out how the girl is doing as well as the man from the other car? Can I get you some cocoa?"

I immediately envisioned Madison, her brow creased with concern, offering me cocoa.

"It's not just the accident. It's not just that someone died and that the girl didn't look much older than Madison." I took a breath, on the edge of revealing something excruciatingly personal to this man I hardly knew. He was in my bedroom, sitting on the edge of my bed. I guess maybe we knew each other better than expected for a landlady and her tenant. "Eli's accident was on that same curve. I haven't driven that road for ten years. The morning I got the call, when I was racing to the hospital because they said he was really bad off and I needed to hurry, that was the last time I drove that road. The car had been towed away, but it looked like someone had set a bomb off on the side of the road. Trees were broken…and there was glass…."

This time his hand stayed on my shoulder. "And the first time in ten years that you work up the courage to drive down that road, you witness a fatal accident. Kay, I'm so sorry."

A tear, hot and wet, rolled down my cheek to splash onto

the comforter. I blinked furiously, trying to get myself under control. "I'll be okay. It's just dredging up a lot of memories that I thought were dealt with and neatly packed away. Maybe cocoa, and some sleep. And yes, if you could find out about the victims, especially the girl."

He continued sitting for a few moments, his hand still on my shoulder as if he were in no hurry to run away from me and the emotional wound I'd just lanced right in front of him. Then he got up and closed my blinds against the morning sun, and left, promising me cocoa and answers.

The cocoa helped, and so did another four hours of sleep. Feeling disoriented to be getting out of bed close to lunchtime, I got my shower and headed downstairs. Taco was napping in the window seat, so content that I knew the kids, or perhaps the judge, had fed him. The house was silent, but some faint sounds from outside had me peeking out my kitchen window where I saw Madison and Chelsea sunbathing while Henry was in the gazebo, his thumbs quick on his phone.

The back door opened, and Judge Beck came in with a burst of warm summer air. "I kicked them out of the house so they wouldn't disturb you. How are you doing?"

"Much better. Thank you for the cocoa and for feeding Taco for me." Then I realized something—it was Tuesday, the day after a holiday, and Judge Beck wasn't at the courthouse. Had he taken the day off as well?

"The kids took care of Taco. And you're welcome for the cocoa. You'll be glad to know that the girl who was in the accident is fine. They kept her overnight for observation on her head injury. Other than that, a fractured arm and some bruises, she's okay. The man in the other car was treated and released with minor injuries. No heart attack—it was just a bruised rib from the seat belt."

I notice he didn't mention about the driver. Although

there wasn't much to say about someone who had died at the scene. I wondered if they even did autopsies on the victims of car accidents? I'm sure it was pretty evident that he died from internal bleeding, or a serious head injury.

*Eli, a crumpled mess of broken bones and cuts, monitors and tubes everywhere. "Love you. See you soon."*

I clenched my teeth, forcing the vision back.

"Here's where it gets weird," Judge Beck continued. "The girl isn't Violet Smith, it's her sister Peony."

I frowned. "But Peony was here with the other girls. We all went to see the fireworks together."

"And she left at eleven with the others, with Maria to be precise."

I thought about that for a moment. It was summer break, and Peony had the reputation of being a party girl, of having very little parental supervision. It was one of the reasons that Judge Beck wasn't crazy about Madison being friends with her.

"She must have gone out to party with some friends and been on her way home," I said, thinking once again about Matt's warning. Drunk driving had nearly claimed two lives last night.

"And the driver? The one who died?" The judge hesitated. "You're not going to believe this, but it was Holt Dupree."

My mouth dropped open. Holt Dupree, our hometown hero, was dead.

## CHAPTER 12

*I* gripped the edge of the counter. "Holt Dupree is dead?" I thought of that young, strong man, that cocky grin and handsome face. He was talented, smart. He had his whole life ahead of him, a glorious future that promised fame and fortune. All of that was taken away early one morning on a sharp curve in a country road.

Judge Beck nodded. "Holt Dupree. I haven't told the kids yet. Chief Danson said they were trying to keep a lid on it until his family and the spokesperson for the Falcons could make a statement. It will probably hit the press this evening at the latest, and I'm sure rumors are already flying."

My brain didn't want to make sense of this. "He was supposed to have left town after the fireworks. Why was he still here, and what was he doing with Peony Smith in his car?"

I had a good idea what he was doing with Peony Smith in his truck at two in the morning and his team's PR person would have had a fit. So much for Daisy's intuition and her informant. It seems that Holt Dupree wasn't as careful about random liaisons and ensuring his partners were of legal age after all. And it wasn't like Peony could have lied to him when everyone in the town knew she was fifteen. Heck, Holt grew up here, in the same neighborhood as she had. He'd dated her older sister. He knew Peony was still in high school without needing to ask anyone.

"As neither her mother or Peony are alleging any wrong-doing, we may never know what she was doing in his car." The judge grimaced. "I can guess, and I'm a horrible person because I'm just glad it wasn't Madison. Accident aside, he shouldn't have been messing around with her. She's still in high school, for God's sake."

Seven years difference wasn't that big of a deal at our age, but in the teen years it was a huge gap. And beyond that, it was illegal. Fifteen was under the age of consent unless the other individual was no more than four years older. In a few months, Peony would have been sixteen, and although that was still far too young to be fooling around with a twenty-two-year-old in my opinion, the relationship would have been legal then.

A few months. It made all the difference in the world in the eyes of the law, but in my somewhat conservative eyes, it made no difference at all.

"He passed me going really fast, and weaving, as if he'd lost control of the truck. He clipped that other car." I thought again of Deputy Pickford's comment. "Was he drunk? He grew up here, he had to have known that road was winding, and that curve dangerous."

It wasn't any easier to excuse him fooling around with a fifteen-year-old girl than driving her around while drunk. What if he'd killed her as well? Or that other man?

"They ran a tox screen since it's a fatality. Chief Danson told me there was alcohol in the truck, but it was hard to tell if the smell was from Holt or Peony or the broken pint of Jack on the floor. We'll have to wait and see."

How the mighty had fallen. And how very quickly Holt had fallen after his recent rise to fame. It was sad to think of what his life might have been, cut short so young. Twenty-two. I was just glad his soul didn't have Peony's death on it as well.

* * *

"I CAN'T BELIEVE he's dead." Madison's eyes were puffy, her nose red. "We had so much fun on the raft at the regatta. He carried me out of the water. I saw him yesterday at the parade on the float with the cheerleaders. How can he be dead?"

*Because sometimes death comes with the swiftness of a bolt of lightning, striking us while we are unprepared and far too young.* Although I could hardly say that to Madison, who was young and scared and looking for some reason why this had happened. I remembered how invulnerable children felt, how death was something that happened to the old. Eventually that innocence was shattered by a schoolmate's death from cancer, or drowning, or some accident. Even I was shaken, and I'd grown somewhat used to death stopping by to take someone I knew—my parents, a friend, my husband. But for a teenager who'd expected to not encounter that grim reaper for many years, this was terrifying.

If Holt Dupree, who was almost a superhero, could die without warning, when his life was in the ascendancy, when everything was going his way, then what faith did Madison have that she would live to see tomorrow? Or that her brother or best friend would live to see tomorrow?

"And Peony...she could have died too," Madison continued. "She was in the car, and she might have died."

Madison's friend. Not a best friend, but still someone who got included in parties and gatherings. That cut even more close to home for the girl. I reached out and smoothed my hand down her glossy dark hair, resting it on her shoulder.

"I know. It's scary, isn't it? I'm glad Peony is okay. And I wish Holt had been okay, too."

"Was he drunk? I mean, he had to have been drunk, right? Chelsea said Holt wasn't drinking at the party on Persimmon Bridge, but he couldn't have had the accident if he wasn't drunk."

I could barely stand that look of fear in her eyes, but I couldn't lie to her. "The police think he might have been drinking but we don't know yet why he had the accident."

"He was at a party, drinking, and missed the turn," she announced confidently.

I remembered the truck passing me, the driver skillfully and confidently cutting back into our lane to take that first curve. He hadn't been weaving. He hadn't been drifting around like I assumed that drunk drivers did. But he was going fast, and on that road, a split second of delayed response, and an overcorrection… There was a broken bottle of whisky in the car, but was Holt Dupree drunk? Had he been drinking, or was the whisky Peony's?

"Madison, many people have car accidents sober. A wet pavement, or a moment of inattention, or lack of sleep, sometimes an accident is an accident." I didn't want to scare her further, but I couldn't confidently say this was alcohol related until the labs and the medical examiner told us so.

"So if I don't drive, and don't drink, and…"

I pulled her into my arms and hugged her tight. "No, you live your life, because worrying and living in fear does nothing to change whatever might be in your future. Don't drink and drive, or take drugs. And when you do drive, drive carefully. Do all those other things smart people do to stay safe, but don't waste your life, whether it's thirty years or ninety years, by living in fear."

"I can't believe he's dead," Madison sobbed into my shoulder.

I rubbed her back, relishing the softness of her dark hair against my face, smelling the apricot-vanilla shampoo she used and for a brief second, imagining that she was my daughter—the child I'd always prayed for but never received.

"I know, sweetie. I know."

Heather came to pick the kids up that night. They filed out in somber silence, Madison's face still tear-stained, her eyes red. I waved them off, then as Judge Beck spread his work out on the dining room table, I vanished into the basement with Taco and my knitting. There I finished my scarf and wrapped it around my shoulders as I snuggled my cat and watched old Will & Grace episodes. Eli's ghost kept me company, hovering just off to the side of the television.

He'd been fifty-two at the time of the accident, sixty-one when he'd died earlier this year. It had been too soon. He'd been too young.

"At least you weren't twenty-two," I told the ghost. As usual, he didn't reply, didn't do more than shift a bit farther left of the TV. Twenty-two. Seven years older than Madison. Nobody should have their life cut off that young, even a cocky, ambitious football player. Nobody.

I turned off the television and carried Taco up to bed, hoping that all the ghosts haunting me—both literally and figuratively—were at rest come morning.

CHAPTER 13

"*Y*ou doing okay?"

J.T. sat his briefcase on his desk and poured a cup of coffee before coming to hover over me. The news of Holt Dupree's death had hit the town hard. It was all over the news by yesterday evening, shared throughout social media with expressions of shock and dismay. The town was in mourning, and I'd bet that section of Jones Road was covered with flowers, letters, and memorabilia. I wouldn't know. I didn't drive that way and didn't plan on doing so ever again.

"Thanks for asking, I'm fine." I turned my chair to face my boss. "Please tell me you're not going to make this into an episode of Gator, Private Eye."

He laughed obligingly at my attempt to keep things light. "Of course not. There's no mystery to solve, no bad guy to catch. Poor kid had too much whisky and missed the turn. Almost took out that oncoming car. Could have killed his passenger. It's a bad road to be driving drunk."

"It's a bad road to be driving sober," I commented, Eli's accident always on my mind lately.

He shook his head. "Dark, moonless night like that. I'm just glad you're okay. And I'm glad you saw where the truck had gone down or that poor Smith girl would have been trapped down there all night."

I shuddered, then looked at J.T. in surprise. "How did you know it was Peony Smith in the passenger seat? None of that was released to the news."

"It's a small town." He grinned. "And I know all the cops, remember?"

Of course I remembered. J.T. was worse than Daisy when it came to knowing all the gossip, although lately I seemed to be running a close third.

"She's fifteen," I mentioned with an arched eyebrow. Yes, I was just as bad of a gossip.

J.T. shrugged. "The girl told the police he was giving her a lift home from a party. Between the head injury and hysterical crying, her statement was a bit disjointed, but I'm guessing any naughty business between the two of them hadn't yet occurred."

Poor Peony. "How is she doing? I heard they kept her overnight for observation because of the head injury?"

J.T. sent me an approving glance. "Your sources are almost as good as mine. They ended up keeping her last night too. Released her this morning to the care of a mother who didn't seem too thrilled about picking her kid up from the ER. Seems she was very worried about who was going to pay for all of it."

I couldn't blame Mrs. Smith for that. They probably didn't have insurance, and hospital visits were horribly expensive—I knew this first hand.

"Pretty serious head wound if they kept her two nights," I commented, remembering that Peony had been unconscious when they'd pulled her from the car.

"Broken arm, concussion, lots of bruises and cuts—some

requiring stitches." J.T. shot me a knowing look. "They breathalyzed her in the hospital. Point o-nine."

Drunk. And probably Holt as well. I frowned. "She's a minor. Could she consent to that? Did they have to wait for her Mom to give the okay?"

He waved a finger at me. "Good catch! If she had been driving, they absolutely could breathalyze her, especially because there is a fatality involved."

"But she wasn't driving," I countered.

"No. So they'd need either a court order, search warrant, consent of the minor, or consent of the parent."

I thought for a moment. "No judge is going to give the okay for that. There's no legal reason to invade her privacy."

"The other allowance is when blood alcohol content is needed for medical evaluation and treatment."

"But then the results are private under HIPAA laws and wouldn't be available to law enforcement except under a court order or search warrant," I countered. "So back to square one. Either she or her mother must have consented."

J.T. chuckled. "We need to get you your PI license. You're good. In this case, Peony declined the breathalyzer. Her mother consented, ranting and railing the whole time that maybe a few weeks in a jail cell would do the girl good."

I winced, feeling even more sorry for Peony. "Why do the police even need to breathalyze her? She wasn't driving. The blood alcohol content of the passenger shouldn't matter in determining cause of the accident. Are they really going to throw a fifteen-year-old girl in juvie after being in a serious accident because she was drinking?"

"Probably not, but it's good to have that information." J.T. sat on the side of my desk. "It's always better to have too much data than too little."

Not always. I thought about jigsaw puzzles, and how the five-hundred-piece ones were so much easier to put together than the three-thousand-piece ones, even if the smaller set was missing pieces. Too much data was overwhelming. It muddied the waters. It made it hard to see the forest for all the millions of saplings.

So says the skip tracer—queen of all data.

It was difficult to get any work done with the accidents—both Eli's and Holt's—on my mind. I read the announcement from the Falcons about how grieved they were over the loss of their newest draft pick, expressing their condolences to both Holt's family and the community. It was well worded, with no mention at all of any suspected cause of the accident or that the deceased had an underage passenger. There was no comment from his family beyond a short depressing interview on News Nine with Holt's mother clutching a picture of him, her eyes empty of life. There was no father, no siblings mentioned at all. Was the poor woman all alone now? It broke my heart to see her in that chair, a microphone shoved in her face.

I was just getting back to my Creditcorp files and thinking about what I might want to do for lunch when I got the call. A nervous girlish voice answered my greeting, asking for me by name. I recognized her voice right away.

"Peony? It's Miss Kay. Oh, honey how are you?"

"They told me you were in the car behind us, that you saw…" She cleared her throat. "They told me you found the truck, that if you hadn't spotted us down the ditch in the woods, we might have been there until dawn. I might have woken up next to…"

A corpse. Trapped in a car, injured and in pain, with the dead body of a boy she knew next to her. I knew where her imagination had gone on this one, and the thought horrified me as well. It wasn't something a fifteen-year-old girl should be imagining.

"Well, that didn't happen," I told her firmly. "And I'm sure the police would have noticed all the broken trees once they finished with Mr. Coleman's statement and the tow truck got there."

"I wanted to thank you." Her voice broke. "Thank you for being there and noticing. And I wanted to ask you to help me. Because I need your help. Please."

I hesitated, then felt like a complete jerk because I was not sure I wanted to know what sort of help a wild girl from the wrong side of the tracks wanted from me—a fifteen-year-old girl who'd been drunk at a party and gone off with an older boy to probably engage in sexual activity.

She was a young girl, just like Madison. I should be willing to assist a girl in need regardless of her background and the poor decisions she'd made.

"What do you need, honey? A written character reference for your underage drinking trial? The name of a good lawyer? Or an alcohol treatment program?"

"I'm not an alcoholic," she snapped back, sounding much more like herself. "I just was partying. Sheesh, you old people are such duds. No, I need you to help me with something. Can you meet me at the coffee shop on third?"

"Now?" Hadn't she just been released from the hospital? With stitches and bruises, and a broken arm? Shouldn't she be home in bed? Suddenly a horrible thought crossed my mind.

"Did your mom kick you out, Peony? Do you need somewhere to stay?" Judge Beck wouldn't be thrilled, but maybe I could put the girl up for the night until we arranged something with child welfare.

"No. I just need to see you. Now. Can you meet me?" Her voice was wavering again, pleading. My chest hurt just hearing it.

"Of course, hon. I'll be right there."

# CHAPTER 14

*P*eony looked forlorn as she sat at the high-top table, her coffee untouched. Her left arm was in a cast, about a third of the right side of her face swollen and bruised. There was a cut with some stitches above one of her eyebrows, and the tangled hair sticking out from under a knit cap made me wonder if she had stitches there as well.

I sat down across from her, preparing to offer some sympathetic words but she spoke first.

"Someone killed Holt."

And now I was speechless. Again I saw the scene, the pickup truck passing me, the headlights, the smashed blood-splattered windshield.

"Oh Peony." It was all I could say. When tragedy struck, everyone wanted someone, or something, to blame, a reason for why it had happened. Madison had clung to the drunk-driving cause that the police had put forth. It seemed Peony was going to blame whoever had given the party, or supplied the alcohol, or not insisted on taking Holt's keys away.

"It's true. I know you don't believe me, but it's true.

Someone killed him." She choked on a sob. "I knew him. We grew up together. I knew him."

She'd been entranced by Holt as had all the young women, dazzled by his smile and flirty attentions, but this girl in front of me seemed so very young—too young for a college grad, an NFL draft pick with his whole future ahead of him, to be fooling around with. Maybe he *had* been innocently giving her a ride home. And maybe someone had been a little over generous with the booze at the party, but at the end of the day, it had been an accident, not murder.

"How are you doing, Peony?" I switched the topic to something other than Holt Dupree and his untimely death.

Her lip trembled and she bit down on it then lifted her chin. "I won't be winning any beauty contests for a while, and it will be twelve weeks before I get the cast off my arm, but at least I'm alive."

"I'm glad you didn't have anything more serious than a broken arm," I told her. "Twelve weeks will be gone before you know it."

She shook her head. "But Holt is dead. And it wasn't his fault. It wasn't."

Was she trying to blame the oncoming car? She'd had a head injury, and been inebriated. Perhaps her memory of what happened wasn't the same as mine.

"Did they tell you I witnessed the accident?" I asked gently. "I wasn't just first on the scene, I saw Holt's truck pass me, saw you guys in the wrong lane when I came around the corner. You were right in the path of an oncoming car." Maybe it would be easier to convince her this wasn't murder if she knew I'd seen it myself.

She nodded. "But you didn't see what went on beforehand. You weren't in the truck with him. We were at a party, and he was giving me a ride home. He was leaving, and knew me, so I asked him for a ride...."

"You were hoping for more than a ride home?" There was a flush on her cheeks, something in her eyes that told me so. Whether Holt was on board with that or not, we'd never know. For some reason I was thinking 'not'. In spite of what Judge Beck had told me about his past trouble, I couldn't see him being such a fool as to risk his future on a fling with a young girl. But then again, many older men had fallen from grace by making the same foolish mistake.

Her smile was sheepish. "Well, yeah. Duh. It's not like I'm going to turn that down."

"He was seven years older than you, Peony. He used to date your older sister. And you're fifteen."

She shrugged. "Seven years isn't a lot, and men don't always think with their big brain when it comes to getting some. It was worth a shot. What's the worst that could happen? Him telling me 'no'?"

The worst that could happen was him telling her 'yes'. Actually the worst that could happen was a horrible car accident with a fatality. She was so lucky to have come out of that one alive. This conversation was highlighting the differences between Peony and the rest of Madison's friends. She suddenly seemed so much older than fifteen. She seemed jaded and a bit ruthless. I now knew why Judge Beck was uneasy about Madison's friendship with her.

But in the end she was a fifteen-year-old girl who had been in a terrible car accident, who had lost a childhood friend. She might be cynical, but she was still a teen, and deserving of my sympathy.

"I know what people are saying," Peony continued. "He wasn't drinking. Holt didn't drink. He wasn't drunk. It was the car. Someone killed him."

I winced. "If he wasn't drunk the labs will prove it—but it still doesn't make his death anything but a horrible accident."

She squirmed. "The labs?"

"He's a local celebrity that died in an accident. The coroner's office will run a tox screen on him to see if alcohol or drugs contributed to the accident."

"But why?" she blurted out. "It's not like they're going to charge him with driving under the influence or something. He's dead."

I winced again at her bluntness. "The M.E. report needs to include that, Peony. It's for the insurance company, or in case there are lawsuits. You're claiming that someone killed him. What if someone else thinks the same, like maybe his mother, and sues? The coroner's office needs to make sure they're thorough."

Tears sparkled in her eyes and her hand shook as she took a sip of her coffee. "But it was the truck. Something was wrong with the truck. That's what killed him."

I thought for a second about the way the truck had jerked into the other lane. "Did you grab the wheel for some reason. Was he falling asleep, and you tried to steer back into the other lane?"

"No! I never touched the wheel." She grimaced and lifted a hand to her head. "And he wasn't drunk. Everyone thinks he was drunk, but he wasn't. Something was wrong with the truck."

"They did find whisky in the car," I told her gently. "You were drinking so he may have seemed sober to you, but that doesn't mean he was. The labs aren't back yet, but the officer at the scene assumed he was intoxicated."

Her eyes blazed. "He wasn't. He was completely sober when he picked me up, and he was drinking water. Yeah, he might have had some alcohol in the car, but he wasn't drinking it and he wasn't drunk. Why won't you believe me? Someone did something to his truck."

How many times had a teenager, or even an adult, hid alcohol in a nondescript container? Spiked soda in the fast food cup. Vodka in a water bottle. I opened my mouth to tell her so, only to shut it with a snap. The deputy had said it was whisky in the car, not vodka. If Holt had poured a bunch of whisky in a clear water bottle, then Peony would certainly have noticed the weird non-water color.

"I really think you should wait until after the labs and the autopsy comes back before you go telling everyone that Holt's death wasn't an accident and that someone tampered with his vehicle."

"I want to hire you to investigate his death. It wasn't an accident," she insisted.

I was beginning to think the hospital should have kept her more than two nights for observation. "Peony, why don't you wait until the M.E. posts his findings before you go hiring J.T. to investigate?"

"I don't want Pierson, I want you," she argued. "You were the one who figured out the mayor killed that woman. Everyone says you're smart. Madison says you're the smartest woman she knows, that you can figure anything out. I know Holt was murdered and I don't want to wait for an autopsy, I want to hire you to find his killer."

Logic wasn't getting me anywhere, but maybe if I humored her and talked through this as if it were one of J.T.'s cases, she'd see the folly in it. *What would Gator do?*

"Okay. We don't know cause of death, so any investigation is going to be pure speculation until we do."

"Someone tampered with the truck," she insisted. "Or maybe someone was in the woods and shot the tire on the truck and we lost control. Something was wrong with that truck."

This was devolving into the land of conspiracy theories. Some had their 'grassy knoll' theory, and Peony had her 'shooter in the woods' theory. There had been no gunshot, but I bit back the argument, not wanting to go down the rabbit hole of silencers or snipers from a mile away that could shoot out the tire of a speeding truck through five acres of woods. Play along. Help the girl feel like she was doing something to help her dead friend. Then get back to the office and the Creditcorp files.

"Step one is motive. What motive would someone have to kill Holt Dupree?" I asked. "He was our hometown hero."

Then I remembered the fight at the concert, Matt's comment about how Buck's season had been ruined taking every hope of a college scholarship with it by an injury that some thought hadn't been an accident. I thought of Judge Beck's concern, and knew that there were probably plenty of fathers out there who were equally, or possibly more, worried about their daughters. Hadn't Kendra jilted her boyfriend when she went off with Holt at the Persimmon Bridge party?

What was I thinking? That Kendra's boyfriend was jealous enough to become a sniper in the woods at two in the morning after the Fourth of July holiday?

"Buck Stanford or his father." Peony ticked off the names on her hand. "They both blame Holt for that football accident in high school. Or Kendra Witt because he told her their little fling was ending the moment he left town. Or Kendra's boyfriend. Or Maury Baggs. Or any of the zillion girls he wouldn't sleep with. Ooo, or Ashley What's-her-name's father. He blames Holt for his daughter's breakdown over those forwarded texts. Yeah, it's been like five years, but maybe Holt being in town stirred up a bunch of old revenge feelings and stuff."

For some reason I had my notepad and pen out. I'd bet the NFL contract *did* rub salt in the wound for Buck and his father, and Holt's presence here in Locust Point might have driven either of them to do something foolish. But the others…I was pretty sure Kendra had known there was a slim-to-none chance of her fling with Holt lasting longer than the weekend, and as much of a stooge as her boyfriend must have felt, killing our local football star seemed an overkill revenge for getting dumped. Besides, I was pretty sure he would have been un-dumped once Holt left anyway. As for Ashley's father, that one was a possibility, especially if Holt had done something while he was here to dredge all of that up again.

"Who is Maury Baggs?" I asked. Lord forbid this actually was a murder because the zillion disappointed, ego-bruised girls weren't going to make for a quick investigation. Although if Holt Dupree were murdered, I wouldn't be the one doing the investigation, the police would.

What was I doing? I needed to placate Peony and go back to work, because this *wasn't* a murder and I wasn't a private investigator.

"Maury Baggs was another neighbor of ours." Peony turned her coffee cup then took a quick drink. "He was a big kid when we were young. Like big. Fat. Bowl full of pudge, fat. Holt was…well, he wasn't nice to him. And he wasn't nice to him in high school either."

My pen paused and I looked up at the girl from under my eyebrows. "Not nice how?"

She had the grace to blush. "Wedgies. Swirlies. Other…things."

It was unbelievable that she hadn't said anything, or moved to defend a poor fat kid who'd been tormented for his entire life. If Holt had been murdered, and this Maury Biggs had done it, I was gonna turn a blind eye and consider it justice done.

"I don't think it's Maury, though. He's still fat and he's more interested in his double-stack with cheese than getting off his sofa and killing someone. No, it's Buck or Kendra."

My pen stopped. "Wait. Kendra, and not her jilted boyfriend?"

"David Tripp." Peony sipped the coffee. "Maybe, but he's kinda whipped. He's more likely to slink off with his tail between his legs and wait to come running when Kendra waves him back. Kendra was convinced she could get Holt to make their booty-call a whole lot more. She wasn't the only one he was banging this weekend, you know. Not that she cared as long as she was the only one who got a call-back for a repeat performance."

I shook my head, completely shocked at all of this. "He's sleeping his way through Locust Point, and Kendra seriously thinks she has a chance to be the one he sticks with?"

"She was working it pretty hard. And Holt's always screwed around. A girl's gotta be willing to turn a blind eye to stuff if she wants to bag a hot dude with money. That's the way it goes."

No, that's most certainly not the way it goes. And I couldn't believe that this fifteen-year-old girl thought so.

"And you liked this guy? This cheating, philandering, bullying, swirly-giving philanderer?"

Peony laughed. "Yeah, of course I like him. Holt grew up in Trenslertown and you learn to do what you gotta do when you live in Trenslertown. Anyway, you can't blame a guy for keeping his options open. Not like he was needing to settle down or anything at his age. Plus, Kendra didn't care one bit what Holt was doing as long as she thought she had a chance of being some athlete's millionaire, Botox wife."

It was a long shot. Why bother to kill a guy when you knew going into it that your chances of him marrying you were probably the same as winning the state lottery, or at the very least the same as winning that Bakery Madness Basket at bingo? But some people had a bit of a screw loose, and who knew what promises Holt had made to her when they were alone and intimate.

What was I thinking? Holt hadn't been murdered. It was an accident, but here I was diving into the investigation. I guess you could never take the reporter out of the reporter, no matter how many years it had been since I'd investigated something beyond debtors or the former owner of my antique sideboard.

"And the millions of girls that Holt said 'no' to? Although from what you're saying, 'no' didn't seem to be a word he used often when it came to women."

Peony ran her fingers through the ends of her long hair. "Not millions. A few girls felt a bit stung that they didn't get to cut a notch on their bedpost with Holt. But if they did something, they probably just meant to hurt him and teach him a lesson. I don't think any of them wanted to actually kill him. Ashley's dad, Kendra, and Buck or maybe his father might have wanted to kill him."

This was ridiculous. Holt Dupree hadn't been murdered. But for some strange reason, I wrote all this down in my notes and handed her my card when I stood, telling her to call me if she had any further information. Should I tell her the rates? That might scare her off pursuing this crazy theory of hers.

Although I didn't even know our rates. J.T. handled all of that, and I just did the research. Besides, I was pretty sure Peony didn't have any money. Hopefully she'd go home, have a good cry, grieve like so many others, and forget about all this in a day or two.

She reached out to grip my fingers with her non-injured hand, crumpling the business card between us. "Thank you. I know I'm just some kid. I know I shouldn't care about Holt, but he was like a brother to me growing up, and I was in that truck too. I could have been killed. And he should have never been killed. It wasn't right. I might not be Locust Point's next valedictorian, or some rich woman, but I know wrong when I see it, and somebody wanted Holt dead. Somebody killed him, and I want that person to go to jail."

$\mathcal{I}$ went back to the office and worked on the two bail cases, gratefully calling it a day and heading home promptly at five. I arrived to an empty house. The kids were with their mom this week. Judge Beck was, no doubt, working late. Taco was practically comatose on the window seat cushion. My mind was whirring with facts and suspicions and crazy thoughts of murder where there was yet to be any proof of such.

I couldn't help thinking of Holt Dupree. I wasn't surprised when a shadow materialized the moment I'd strolled through my front door. I was so used to Eli's ghostly presence in the house that I passed by it and went into the kitchen, doing a quick inventory and throwing myself into cooking before I realized the ghost at my door wasn't what— or who— I'd thought.

It wasn't Eli. I pulled the veggies out of the fridge and put a pot on to boil as the shadow slunk into my kitchen to lurk near the pantry. This ghost felt different. Male, but not that comforting presence that I got around the spirit I'd come to associate with my husband. This one felt younger and annoyed.

It felt like the ghost at the accident scene the other night. In fact, I was sure it was the same ghost I'd seen there.

I didn't personally know Holt Dupree, but since the other ghosts appeared after I'd seen a dead body, or a beloved piece of furniture that they'd owned, I assumed this new specter was our local football star. When I'd seen the shadowy form at the scene of the accident, I'd assumed it was some sort of temporary manifestation, and that it would remain an hour or so after death until the soul moved toward the light or whatever happened when someone died.

Why had this spirit lingered? And why was it in my house? Was Peony right? Had the accident that took Holt's life really been murder? All the other ghosts were either murdered or associated with a murder. Maybe Holt had killed someone or he knew about a murder and his soul wouldn't rest until I'd uncovered it. If so, he'd be waiting a long time. It had been difficult enough to dig up Mabel's family secrets. I'm sure Holt's would take me the rest of my life to untangle.

I put a container of frozen beef broth into the pot with the water, and started chopping veggies. "I'd like you to get out of my house," I told the ghost. "You're not welcome here. Go haunt someone else, like whoever threw that party and served you too much alcohol."

The ghost moved close enough that I shivered from the chill. I refused to look at him, instead concentrating on my carrots. That's when I noticed the potato rocking side to side, then rolling forward off my counter and onto the floor.

My knife froze mid-chop. The spirits I'd seen in the past didn't speak, and they didn't move stuff around. I told the ghost of Holt to cut it out, picked up the potato and washed it before continuing my chopping.

The potato rolled off the counter again.

"Fine." I slapped the knife on the counter and jammed my hands on my hips. "You want my attention? You've got it. What do you want?"

Nothing. Well, nothing beyond that shadowy blur and the unusual cold spot. And the strange sensation that the ghost was irritated. I didn't blame him. He was dead at twenty-two. He'd never play for the Falcons, get the Nike contract, marry that supermodel. I'd be angry too.

"Were you killed, or are you just mad because you're dead?" I asked, knowing full well that the ghost wasn't going to respond. "Because if it's the first, then the police will handle it. If it's the second, well I'm sorry, but there's nothing I can do about that."

Anger. Frustration. Yeah, I was frustrated too. This would be the third time I'd washed this potato. I stopped down to pick it up, deciding to wait until I was ready to chop it before washing it yet again. Good thing too as once more it took a dive for the floor, this time rolling around a can of lima beans and a package of frozen corn on its way off the counter. I scooped my chopped carrots into the stock pot, picked up the potato and washed it, gripping it firmly as I diced it to make sure it didn't leap from my hands to the floor.

A can wobbled, tipping onto its side. I reached out and grabbed it. "Cut it out. One more thing hits the floor and I'm calling Olive to have her banish you. She's a medium. She does that kind of thing."

I wasn't sure she did. I knew she did séances. I also knew that she was the Accounting Manager for Smoky Hollow Land Development Corp, that she preferred her wines on the sweet side, that she dragged a canvas and easel out in the middle of fields one weekend each month to do plein air paintings, and that her dream vacation was a riverboat cruise down the Rhine, but I didn't know if she could banish ghosts. Olive had become one of our Friday happy-hour-on-the-porch gang, and I really liked her. Even if she couldn't get rid of this pesky poltergeist, I knew she'd come help me out if I asked. And I knew that nobody, living or not, stood a chance against Olive when she got that determined set to her jaw.

To express the serious nature of my threat, I waved my knife menacingly at the shadow. I don't know if it was Olive or my cutlery, but the ghost vanished, leaving my kitchen warm and sunny as before. I sighed, grateful that he was gone, and returned to my soup.

I tossed in the potatoes, canned lima beans, green beans, and peas along with the frozen corn and a bottle of tomato juice. A dash of Worcestershire and some black pepper, and there was nothing to do but wait for the carrots and potatoes to cook. I eyed a new knitted scarf pattern I wanted to try, but decided to make some cornbread instead.

Sweet cornbread, moist to the point that it was almost a cake, or a spicy, southwestern variety? Hmm. I eyed the stock pot and decided to compromise and do a more traditional style with a hint of gritty cornmeal and actual bits of corn. Within twenty minutes, I had the cornbread in the oven and was once more eyeing my knitting.

Might as well give it a try. If I was lucky, I wouldn't have to tear it all out. I was about to gather up my yarn and needles, when Taco came meandering into the kitchen, yawning with a feigned casualness. Sneaky boy. I put the lid on the soup just to make sure I didn't return to find my cat face-down in the stock pot, and gave the counter a quick swipe. The cat sat at my feet and meowed at me, waving an adorable paw at his food bowl.

"Not yet, sweetie," I told him. He gave me the most pitiful, starving kitty look. I swear that cat was A-list when it came to acting ability.

And I was a sucker. I dug a couple of kitty treats from the jar, scooped up my knitting, and headed into the parlor with a chirping cat dancing at my feet. Taco snatched the treats as if he hadn't been fed in weeks, then curled up at my side, rubbing his head along my thigh as I concentrated on the deceptively simple scarf pattern. Worried that I'd mess up the eyelet pattern, I carefully counted stitches each row and was thrilled to have added nearly two inches to the project by the time my timer beeped for the cornbread.

The yarn went on a shelf, safe from a very interested Taco. The cornbread went into the pie safe, away from the cat's clutches. Then I tested my carrots and potatoes and found them to be done.

One more step. I pulled a small head of cabbage out of the fridge and shredded a few cups, stirring them into the soup before replacing the lid. Five minutes. Just enough to wilt the cabbage, and dinner would be ready. It didn't give me enough time to do any further knitting, but I did manage to slice the cornbread and put the steaming hot pieces onto a plate.

I was just ladling the soup into a bowl when I heard the front door open. I sat the bowl aside and pulled another one from the cupboard hearing heavy footsteps on my creaky, old wooden floors. Judge Beck poked his head in and sniffed. He was holding a plastic grocery-store bag in one hand and a DVD in another.

"Dinner is served," I told him. "Hope you like vegetable soup and cornbread."

"I do." He pulled a quart of cookie-dough ice cream from the bag and stuck it into the freezer. "This is for later. As is the movie. How are you doing?"

I almost told him about the ghost that had been taking out his temper on my potato— the ghost that had returned to hover over his shoulder, the one that wasn't Eli, but then I saw the movie he'd brought home. "Blazing Saddles?"

"A good comedy cures all evils. Besides, it's one of my favorites."

It was one of Eli's favorites as well. He'd loved Mel Brooks movies. A couple times a year we would sit through marathons of them, pausing the movies only to go pee or microwave some popcorn. Then we'd debate which was the best. I'd always been partial to Young Frankenstein, where Eli was a fan of Spaceballs.

Ice cream and a movie? I handed Judge Beck his bowl of soup and a small plate with a piece of cornbread on it and wondered if this was what all tenants did when their landlord had witnessed a fatal car accident. Although Judge Beck and I were kind of beyond the tenant/landlord relationship. He'd been living here less than six months and I saw him as family, as much of a best friend as Daisy was.

"I'm still a bit shaken," I told him as I followed him into the dining room with my bowl and plate in hand. "I purposely drove by the accident site tonight even though I swore I'd never go that way again. I just wanted to see it in the daylight and try to disconnect the tragedy of what happened last night from Eli's accident ten years ago."

The judge arched an eyebrow at me. "You don't wait around, do you? Just rub that salt right into the open wound."

I shrugged. "Not salt, antiseptic. Clean it out so it can heal." I wasn't sure how to explain to him that I needed to break the cycle of grief the accident had plunged me into. I'd been spiraling downward, churning up all the memories and pain that I'd thought I'd buried long ago. It was one thing to mourn a young life lost, but I just couldn't go through all that pain over Eli's accident again. I couldn't relive that horrible morning, those weeks of agony beside his bed in the hospital, the months when I slowly began to realize that the Eli I loved was never coming back.

I hadn't dealt with it then, and I wasn't ready to deal with it now. So I stuffed it all down and thought about Holt Dupree, about his ghost that had trailed behind us from the kitchen to drift around the dining room table.

Leave it to Holt Dupree to follow me home, toss a potato around my kitchen, and intrude on my dinner like this. Why couldn't he just stay at the scene of the accident or haunt his childhood house? It was beyond rude to be hanging around my house.

"Did it help?"

It took me a second to realize what Judge Beck was referring to. Oh. The site of the accident.

"A bit. Eli's wreck was in the same spot, so I can't say I was able to separate the two as easily as I'd hoped. What did help was going back to work today. It's my routine. And it's comforting."

His smile was warm, with little creases at the corners of his eyes. "Good. Lots of debtors to track down? A few bail jumpers and repossessions to keep things lively?"

"Just the bad debt research today." I chuckled, remembering that my day had more than the usual Creditcorp files. "Oh, there was one unusual request. I'm not just a skip tracer now, I'll have you know. I received a phone call this afternoon from someone. Evidently I have a new client who has requested me to personally investigate a case for her."

This time both of the judge's eyebrows rose. "Should I get your autograph now? Maybe steal your shopping lists so I can sell them on eBay when you're famous? Gator is going to get jealous when your YouTube videos surpass his in terms of views."

"Oh, I'm not Gator Pierson, but I am now hired by Peony Smith to investigate the accident that injured her and caused

Holt Dupree's death. I doubt she has any money to pay me with, though. Which is just as well since I'm not a licensed private investigator anyway."

The spoonful of soup paused halfway to his mouth. "Peony Smith? She's a high school kid."

"Even high school kids deserve justice," I told him solemnly.

He ate a few bites of soup, then shook his head. "So does she think she's going to sue Holt's estate for damages if it turns up he was drunk? The guy just signed his contract. I doubt if he's got more than a few thousand in his checking account. He was just starting practice next week."

"No, I don't think she's trying to get any money out of the deal. She thinks someone killed him, that the wreck wasn't an accident."

The judge stared at me in disbelief. "You're joking. He was a local hero. He didn't have any money, or even any real fame yet. Does she think someone forced a pint of vodka down his throat and stuck him behind the wheel because they were jealous?"

"Maybe. No, actually she's convinced either someone sabotaged the truck, or a sniper shot out their tire from the woods."

He shook his head. "And who are the main suspects in this crazy set of theories?"

"One is Ashley Chen's father, Robert."

"After five years he snaps and kills Holt Dupree by messing with his car? Or by buying him a few rounds and putting him behind the wheel?"

Yeah, it didn't sound very believable. "How about Buck Stanford? He got into an altercation with Holt at the concert. Or that Kendra Witt who was his weekend squeeze and hoped to be more, only to be dumped after the fireworks? Or Maury the swirly kid."

"Who in the world is Maury Swirly?" Judge Beck shook his head. "Not that it matters. Kay, please tell me you don't seriously believe any of these people killed Holt Dupree. It was an accident, whether or not alcohol was involved."

I put a hand up. "I know, I know. I felt sorry for Peony, though. She's been in a horrible car accident, and she grew up with him. Holt was a neighbor. He used to date her older sister. He was that poor kid who made it big, and now he's dead and she was in the truck when it happened. She's hurt and grieving and she wants to blame somebody. I completely understand."

He set his spoon down and eyed me. "Did you want to blame someone when Eli had his accident?"

I winced as the pain speared through me. Then I forced it down, back into the little place where I hid all the things that were too hard to face.

"Yes, I did. I blamed myself, the hospital, his patient that needed the surgery that brought him in that morning, the idiots who designed that road with a horrible sharp curve in it. I blamed him, I blamed God. And when he died this year, I wanted to blame everyone all over again. Why hadn't his doctors known he was going to have a stroke? Why hadn't I seen the signs? Why hadn't Eli—a doctor for Pete's sake—seen the signs? Yes, I wanted to blame somebody. It was easier to think it was all someone else's fault than face the fact that horrible things happen to good people for absolutely no reason at all."

Judge Beck's gaze softened. "So you took Peony's case."

I stared down at my soup. "I'm not a licensed investigator. She's a teenager from a poor family, and couldn't afford to hire an investigator anyway, even if I did have a license."

"You took her case." His voice was gentle, as if he completely understood why I'd agreed to check up on Peony's claims, investigator license or not.

"Yes, I took her case. I tried to reason with her, but then I realized that the best thing I could do for the girl was give her hope. I'll nose around and check a few things until the lab results come back on his blood alcohol level, or drugs or anything else in his system. It won't hurt me to do a little research while we wait for the official cause of death. Then maybe Peony will be ready to hear the news that nobody killed Holt Dupree, that it was either a tragic accident, like what happened with Eli, or he'd partied too hard and should have never been driving, let alone giving her a lift."

Judge Beck broke off a piece of his cornbread. "You're a good woman, Kay."

I felt myself blush. No, it was probably just a hot flash, although I hadn't had one of those for a few months. Yes, definitely a hot flash.

"Thanks. And I appreciate you thinking to bring home the movie and the ice cream."

He smiled, and once again it crinkled up the corners of his eyes. "The kids are with their mom, so what do you say about following up Blazing Saddles with some Young Frankenstein?"

"I'd say 'yes'."

Taco jumped on the table and stared pointedly at my cornbread. I fed him the remains of my piece, completely breaking my rule about not giving the cat any human food, let alone the rule about letting him up on the table. Blazing Saddles, Young Frankenstein, and a huge tub of cookie dough ice cream. It was shaping up to be a pretty good night after all.

# CHAPTER 16

The next morning I was busy pulling arrest records and waiting for the folks at Creditcorp to get back to me on a skip trace when J.T. walked through the door with Deputy Miles Pickford right behind him.

"You doing okay, Kay?" he asked.

I must be doing okay because I was getting tired of people asking me that question and acting as though I was some fragile creature on the edge of collapse because I'd been first on scene of a fatal accident.

"Good. There's lemon muffins by the coffee maker. Help yourself."

He made haste toward the coffee maker. J.T. had already snagged two of the muffins when I'd first brought them in, and looked like he was deciding whether to indulge in second breakfast or not.

"Holt Dupree." Miles shook his head, crumbs falling to the floor as he took a bite of the muffin. "Dude was far too young to die. And drunk driving too. Not that anyone should be surprised. Those folks from Trenslertown aren't exactly known to be sober, law-abiding citizens."

I bristled at the stereotype of our less fortunate citizens, but Miles and the other officers saw the worst of society on a regular basis. It must be hard to look on the sunny side when every day he had to face domestic violence complaints, drunk and disorderly calls, and drug deals gone bad. Judge Beck probably had the same difficulty in having faith in humanity.

"He was drunk then? The labs came in?" J.T. asked.

That would have been really fast. I knew from J.T. that everything in the county went to Milford where one poor tech had to manage on her own, sending the more complicated analysis to the state lab. A vehicle fatality like this wouldn't be a priority.

"Heck no. We might get them along with the M.E. findings by Friday if we're lucky. If he hadn't been DOA, we could have breathalyzed him and been done with it."

I wasn't so sure about that. The ambulance EMT wasn't likely to allow Miles to breathalyze a critically injured patient, and hospitals were touchy about allowing tests without consent or a court order. Miles, or the detective on the case, would have most likely had to subpoena the hospital records to get the blood alcohol numbers, and *that* would have taken far longer than five business days.

Either way, I was feeling like a bit of a devil's advocate today. "Witnesses at the Persimmon Bridge party say Holt wasn't drinking then. People who know Holt say he didn't drink alcohol. That he didn't want to do anything that might jeopardize his contract and career."

Miles took another bite of the muffin and continued with his mouth full. "What twenty-two-year-old guy *doesn't* drink? The girl was drunk. There was a broken bottle of whisky in the car. Everyone is just making him out to be a saint because he's dead. That guy was no saint, though. Screwed every girl in town, clawed his way to the top no matter who he trampled underfoot."

At the words a shadowy figure materialized by the coffee maker, knocking a thankfully empty cup onto the ground. Miles turned around and frowned at it, then bent to pick it up, shivering as his shoulder passed through the shadow. "What do you have the AC set at, J.T.? Sheesh, it's freezing in here."

"Probably your blood sugar taking a nose dive," J.T. teased. "Better eat another muffin."

Miles took him seriously and reached for another, shivering as his arm passed through the shadowy figure. Another cup hit the floor.

"Klutz," J.T. scoffed. This time it was him that reached down to grab the cup, his arm also passing through the shadow. "Dang, it *is* cold in here."

*That guy was no saint, though. Screwed every girl in town, clawed his way to the top no matter who he trampled underfoot.* Maybe Peony was right. The guy did seem to be leaving a lot of disgruntled folks in his wake. It wouldn't hurt to check out her allegations of foul play.

"Hey Miles, where did Holt Dupree's truck get towed?" I asked, as the deputy filled a cup with coffee and grabbed yet another muffin.

Holt probably had been drunk. But that night when I'd given my statement, I'd thought otherwise. And there was a ghost, one who was perpetually angry and knocking stuff off tables and counters with maddening regularity. Plus, I felt like I should be doing something to investigate Peony's allegations. Her comments about the truck bothered me, like a burr that had worked its way into my sock. She'd said that it seemed to be out of control. Maybe, just maybe there was something wrong with the truck. And whether it was tampering or a manufacturing defect, whether Holt had taken a few shots out of that whisky bottle or not, I felt like I should check it out.

As of now, the death was an accident, and there was no reason to hold the truck for evidence. I assumed Holt's mother would be pulling it out of impound as quickly as she could to avoid paying a fortune in fees, but the insurance company would need to look at it. Plus, there wasn't anything worth salvaging in that truck from what I recalled seeing that night. Ms. Dupree would pull it from impound. The insurance company would take their pictures. Then off it would go to the junkyard. I didn't think there was anything in Peony's accusations, but it was worth a trip to the tow yard.

Not that I knew much about cars. I could possibly bribe one of the guys at the tow yard to look at it for me. I didn't have much in the way of money, and I was pretty sure Peony wouldn't be able to reimburse me for these sorts of expenses. Hopefully the guy at the tow yard would take the promise of strawberry cream-cheese muffins as an adequate bribe.

"Doug's Towing picked it up," Miles told me. "He's got a yard out on East past Twelfth Street. Why? Are his folks looking to claim it? They're better off just letting the insurance company release it to a salvage yard. It's totaled."

"Has the insurance company been out yet?" I'd better hustle or the pickup would be a square of squashed metal by the time I got there.

"Probably not. It usually takes them three or four days, although they might have hurried this one up because of the publicity. Usually they photograph it when there's a fatality and a passenger with injuries." Miles shoved the rest of the muffin in his mouth. "After that Doug will need to keep it until Holt's folks sign off on it. Then he'll strip it, and if the frame isn't worth saving, he'll have to wait for the truck to haul it off. His yard doesn't have a crusher."

Good. That meant I had some time. I jotted down Doug's Towing in my notebook and looked at what I'd written during my conversation with Peony. Kendra Witt. Boyfriend David Tripp. Buck Stanford. Robert Chen. I pulled out a piece of paper and ordered them by likelihood based on motive. Then I drew a line and added Violet Smith to the list as a possible source of information. I stared at my list and frowned. Motive, but unless I knew cause of death, motive wasn't going to get me anywhere. I drew another line and added possible causes of death. Trauma due to vehicle accident: Inattention. Interference by passenger. Falling asleep. Unknown medical condition such as epilepsy or stroke. Alcohol or drugs. Animal in the road. Pavement conditions. Automotive failure—either defect or sabotage.

Mr. Coleman would have mentioned an animal in the road, as would Peony, so I crossed that one off. Without the lab results and M.E. findings, the only thing left for me to check out was pavement conditions and automotive failure.

I hadn't said anything to J.T. about this little side job of mine. Peony wouldn't be able to pay, and I wasn't licensed to officially investigate this, but there was no reason a nosy woman couldn't check a few things out on her lunch hour.

Starting with Doug's Towing.

$\mathcal{D}$oug was younger than I'd expected—late thirties with a powerful build, a long torso, and bright blue eyes. His hair was somewhere between shaved bald and a military buzz cut. It looked like he had a five-o'clock shadow on the top of his head. He shot me a narrowed glance when I asked if I could possibly see Holt Dupree's truck.

"Unless you're from either the insurance or wrecking company, the answer is 'no'. I've been fending off groupies all day. Last girl here had a bouquet of flowers and a pair of underwear she wanted to leave on it."

"Do I look like a groupie?" I spread my arms wide and turned around, just so he could get a good look at the sixty-year-old woman he was talking to.

Doug grinned. "No. But you don't look like an insurance adjuster either, and I don't see no flatbed out in my lot. Come back with a clipboard in your hand, and I'll let you see it."

I pulled out a bag of muffins and handed them to the guy, feeling like I was doing something illegal.

He shot me a perplexed look and opened the bag. "Is this a bribe?"

"Yes?" I smiled hopefully.

He sighed and went to close the bag, then changed his mind and pulled out a muffin before setting it aside. "Why do you want to see Holt Dupree's pickup anyway? It's wrecked. It still smells like whisky. And there's…well, let's just say I haven't cleaned it."

I remembered going to look at Eli's car. Carson had been kind enough to go with me as I went to pull anything personal from the glove box and CD player, and sign it away. It had been tough. I was pretty sure seeing Holt Dupree's truck was going to drag all of those memories back to the surface. Going by the accident scene yesterday after work had been difficult enough. I knew the moment I saw this vehicle, I'd be seeing the twisted piece of metal that used to be Eli's car with the shattered windshield and rust-colored stains of his blood all over the dash and upholstery. I'd mesh the two incidents together and put myself on the edge of a panic attack.

But I needed to do this. I needed to put the past into the past, and think of this as a case, and myself as some amateur private investigator, digging around for clues like a sixty-year-old Nancy Drew.

I took a deep breath, and decided to level with Doug. "He passed me on Jones Road right before that curve. I saw the accident. I was first on the scene. I was the one who discovered the truck down in the trees. Before that, we all thought it was a hit-and-run and he was long gone. I…I was there."

Doug sat the muffin down. "That's all the more reason for you not to see it."

I took a steadying breath. "The girl that was in the truck with him? She's a friend of a friend, and she's not in a good place right now. She didn't escape that accident unscathed, either physically or emotionally. She swears up and down that something was wrong with the car."

"And you believe her?"

I was glad Doug hadn't rejected the wild idea out of hand. This guy might end up with another half dozen muffins if he kept this up.

"I care about her enough to want to check it out. And in all honesty, I didn't think Holt looked like he was driving like a drunk. It seemed more like how someone would drive if they lost control on an icy road, or had a tire blow, or their power steering broke." I shrugged. "I'm not a mechanic. There's probably nothing I can tell from looking at the truck myself, but I want to take a peek before it gets crushed."

Doug eyed the muffin and picked it up with a sigh. "Okay, lady. Let's go look at the truck."

I followed him around to the gates and stood quietly as he unlocked them.

"You said you're with Pierson's Investigative and Recovery Services? As in Gator Pierson?" he asked, pulling the chain through the links, and swinging the massive metal gate open with a squawk.

"I'm a skip tracer there. This isn't an official investigation or anything. I'm not a licensed investigator. I'm just doing this for the girl, to help her out." Then I thought of something. "Do you watch J.T.'s videos? His Gator series of vlogs?"

Doug shot me a grin over his shoulder and lead me into the yard. "Yeah, everyone in town watches those. He's hysterical, and it's cool to see people you know in the videos. My neighbor was a heroin dealer in episode eight. Do you think...if that girl turns out to be right and there was something wrong with the truck, is Gator going to make this case in to one of his shows?"

"It's not a case—" Oh. Now I realized where Doug was going with all of this.

"You'll absolutely be in that video, especially if you're the one who finds out there was something wrong with the car. Reenactment, plus an interview about your assistance in the case, no doubt."

That seemed to be far more of a motivation to Doug than the muffin bribe, although he was making happy noises as he ate the one he'd carried with him. We wove down wide paths of wrecks choked with weeds and came to a newer section with mangled cars on a cleared strip of gravel-imbedded dirt. The vehicles were neatly positioned in lines with plenty of room between them to get hand-trucks, engine stands, and carts in without banging into the cars next to them. Several were already missing hoods, gaping holes where engines, radiators, and transmissions had once been. A few had been stripped of body panels and interiors. It was clear from looking at these wrecks that used car parts was a productive business.

And as Holt's pickup truck came in to view, it was clear there wasn't much in the way of used parts that would be salvageable from this wreck. Doug stopped and we stood before the smashed vehicle, honoring it and the driver who'd lost his life with a moment of silence.

"It's gonna be hard to see if there was any mechanical problem," Doug said. "Lots of damage from going down in that ditch and through a couple of trees. Looks like it rolled over too, from the dent in the hood."

"Let's start with any kind of mechanical problem that might have caused Holt to lose control of the car. Blown tire?" I suggested.

Doug scratched his head, the muffin already devoured. "Modern tires don't really go like that unless someone runs over a spike strip. Punctures and scrapes usually result in slow leaks. If he hit a curb or something sharp, the tire still wouldn't blow. It would take a few minutes to deflate and he'd have warning and time to get over."

"Even at speed and around a sharp corner?"

The man made his way slowly around the truck, bending over to look at the tires as he walked. "Maybe. It's hard to steer on a tire low on air. Could have affected his reaction time. If he was wide in that corner, with a near-flat he might not have gotten the truck back into his lane in time."

I followed Doug, mimicking his stooped perusal of the tires. There was dirt and stone encrusted along the wheel well and imbedded in the treads. I didn't see any big gashes in the sidewalls, or holes.

Doug stood. "This truck is pretty new, and the tires are sound. Lots of tread. None of them seem flat."

"So not the tires," I confirmed.

"Not the tires," Doug repeated. "Gonna look at the power steering pump and see if something happened with that. Hoses too. If that system loses fluid or seizes up it can happen fast, and a truck with no power steering ain't no picnic to control."

I took my notebook out and jotted down a few things, grateful that Doug was assisting. I didn't know a power steering pump from…well, from any other part of the truck.

It took Doug a while to get to the inside of the truck. The hood needed to be removed in a procedure that involved a crowbar and a hammer, which involved a few trips back to the office while I stood by the wreck and tried not to look at the inside where someone had died, the inside that would be covered with glass and broken plastic and twisted metal and blood, just like Eli's car had been.

"Power steering pump is crushed, and I doubt that happened before the accident. Looks like it was functional before. I'd need to pull all the hoses and belts and look at them, but I'm not sure it would tell me much. There's bound to be cracked and broken hoses and belts from the accident itself and I don't think I can make a determination about whether the damage was because someone poked a hole or cut partway through a belt or if the radiator fan cut through it when the truck hit the trees."

"So…maybe?" I made a note, just in case.

"Maybe. You gonna go by the accident scene at all?" Doug's head popped up out of the truck's engine compartment.

"Yes, I plan on it." I really, really didn't want to, but I needed to check to see if there was anything in the road that might have contributed to the accident, like a giant boulder, or a dead elephant.

"Look for fluid on the road. We haven't had any rain, so it should be there if the pump or a hose gave way—either power steering or brakes. Look for that a quarter mile in to where he went off the road, and if you see something, check it. Power steering fluid and brake fluid should be slippery to the touch. If it's oil, that's not good but it wouldn't cause him to wreck. Or greenish, syrupy-smelling radiator fluid, or gasoline either."

I seriously needed to bring this guy more muffins. I probably needed to buy him dinner by this point.

"Thanks. Got it." I scribbled in my notepad while Doug's head vanished again into the engine compartment.

"Brakes might cause loss of control as well," Doug's muffled voice continued, "especially on a road like that. If he passed you going fast, then tried to slow to take the corner and found he'd lost his brakes, that could have been the swerving you saw."

"And brakes can go just like that?" I asked, remembering what he'd said about the tires.

"Yep. Actually that's a likelier cause than the power steering going out. I can't tell you the number of wrecked cars I've had to pick up because a hose blew in their brake system. The fluid is under pressure, so when it goes, it goes. Bam! Suddenly you have no brakes at all. The parking brake is on a different system, but when you're trying to slow for a traffic light or a curve, you don't usually have much time to think of engaging your parking brake."

This guy was a gem. Even if this turned out to be nothing more than a tragic alcohol-related accident, this was fascinating information.

"Okay. I'll check for fluid in the roadway," I promised.

Doug's head appeared again. "Brake system looks intact. I'll yank off the tires and take a look at the pads to see if there's anything wrong there, although that's not likely to cause your accident. Pad comes loose and your braking makes a horrible noise and gets wonky. It might pull you to the side, but I can't see it causing a complete loss of control."

My lunch hour was quickly turning into two hours, and I hadn't even gone by the accident scene yet. Doug slid under the front left wheel of the truck while I debated telling him not to bother. J.T. had always allowed me to have a somewhat flexible schedule. I could just work late tonight, or even come in early tomorrow. Honestly, I was at a bit of a standstill until the Creditcorp folks got back to me on that one file anyway. I might as well stay and learn about brake pads and the different things that could go wrong with them.

Doug made a yelp noise from under the truck. I squatted down to eye him, alarmed that he may have cut himself on some jagged piece of metal.

Excited brown eyes met mine. "Tie rods. Suspension. This is it."

I had no idea what he was talking about, but clearly it was something big. Doug scooted out from under the truck while I backed up to give him room.

"Vehicle suspension is set up so the wheels can turn in

and out and allow for a degree of torsion. It's a system that improves handling. There's struts and shocks and bearings and joints that all need to be greased and maintained. Older cars have failures and if someone's been sloppy about maintenance, then there can be a failure and suddenly there's no way to control the wheels. A rod can break off, and the wheels aren't lined up properly and you lose control, and if you're going fast and there's a curve, then you're gonna go over the edge."

Doug was talking a hundred miles an hour, his words mashing together as he gestured wildly. All I got out of it was that some rod thing in the suspension sometimes breaks, then like the old cartoons, the driver finds himself holding a steering wheel that doesn't do anything to control the car.

"You're saying this rod is broken?"

He nodded vigorously. "Driver's side front wheel. The tie rod is broken. If it's weak, all it takes is for the tire to hit a curb, or be under strain from going around a tight corner at speed, and it will snap. Once it snaps, there's no way to control the car. You're steering the other wheels, but this one keeps yanking the car in the other direction. This happens, and you're looking at a serious accident. It's why mechanics check for fatigue when they pack the bearings or are replacing the tie rod ends. This kinda thing happens in old cars."

I frowned at the wreck. "But this truck is only a few years old at most."

"Yeah, which means either there was a manufacture defect, or something happened to it. If the truck was in a major accident, and the mechanics fixing it didn't check, they could have missed a damaged tie rod. Or..." Doug gave me a smug grin. He was practically hopping up and down.

"Or someone tampered with it?" I assumed that what he was getting at. "How can someone do that? You said it would take a major accident, so I assume these tie rods aren't the sort of thing than can be easily damaged."

"All it takes is a torch. Someone who knows what they're doing, someone with a welding set and ten or twenty minutes can cut far enough through the tie rod so that with any kind of stress it will break. Could break the same night. Could be a week later. Could be a month later."

I stared at him. It seemed unbelievable that someone would have deliberately sabotaged Holt Dupree's car. "It seems more likely that it was a manufacturing defect, or a bad repair from a previous accident," I told him.

"It would, except I can clearly see where the metal was cut through." Doug gave me a self-satisfied, grim smile. "Clear as day. That's no inherent weakness in the metal. That's no bend from a previous accident. That's cut through with a torch, that's what that is."

Which meant 'that' was murder.

CHAPTER 18

*D*eputy Miles Pickford scooted out from under the wrecked pickup and brushed his hands off on his pants. "I'm not a mechanic, but it does look like someone tampered with the truck. The questions now are 'who', 'how', 'when', and 'why'."

Indeed, those *were* the questions. I'd immediately called in the police once Doug found the cut tie rod, and had been surprised to see they'd sent Miles out instead of a detective from homicide. Although without a cause of death, it might be premature to do anything but claim the tampering was any more than a contributing cause.

"*How* is easy," Doug told him. "You can tell by the edges and the color around the sliced section that someone used a blow torch. Looks like they cut almost the entire way through it. It's a clean cut aside from the small broken portion where it gave way."

Miles put his hands on his hips. "How long do you think it would have held, being cut like that? I'm trying to figure out timing here—if it was cut in the last few days, or if Holt was driving around with it like that for weeks, or months."

132

Doug scratched his nose and frowned. "It's hard to tell. With careful driving it might have held for a few weeks."

"Can't have been," I chimed in. "There was the party at Persimmon Bridge, and parking there is all off-road in the flood plain. You said it would have given way if he'd hit a pothole or a curb, well driving through that flood plain to park would have been the equivalent of a field of potholes."

"True." Doug nodded. "So it happened after that party. Or possibly during it, although I doubt the tie rod would have held getting out of there and back on the road."

"There's no way someone crawled under this truck and took a blow torch to the undercarriage while it was parked in that flood plain," Miles argued. "The grass there is up to my knees and we haven't had rain in two weeks. The whole field would have gone up in flames."

"The Persimmon Bridge party was Saturday night," I mused. "Sunday was the regatta. Then Monday, the parade, fireworks at the carnival grounds, and whatever parties Holt went to before driving Peony home."

"So as for the 'when', we're looking at Sunday or Monday the Fourth." Miles put his hand on the quarter panel of the truck and bent down to peer underneath. "What's your best guess, Doug?"

Doug looked thrilled at his 'expert' status. This was clearly the highlight of his year, if not of his entire adult life. "I'd guess it was done not much before when he had the accident. I'd say Monday night, but there's always a chance someone did it on Sunday and Holt just didn't drive much that day."

"We'll need to trace what Holt did those two days and where the truck was parked," I told Miles. "It's not like a guy blow-torching under a parked truck isn't going to be noticed. It had to be a time when the vehicle was parked in an out-of-the-way place—and a place where the person doing this wasn't likely to set a field on fire."

"And probably during the day," Doug said. "'Cause at night, someone is gonna notice sparks from the torch pretty far away. Might be easy to crawl under the truck under the cover of night, but people would see the sparks from the torch and know something was going on."

"Not on the Fourth of July," I countered. "The carnival grounds had a gravel parking area as well as the field spots, and people were setting off mini fireworks and sparklers near their cars."

I knew this because Judge Beck had been horrified and glad that we'd walked and his SUV wasn't in danger of getting burn marks from a rogue roman candle.

"But was Holt Dupree at the fireworks?" Miles asked. "And did he park there?"

I could tell by his expression that he was dreading the amount of legwork this was going to take. Figuring out when and where the tampering took place would require a ton of interviews, and that didn't even begin to address *who* might have done this.

Miles turned to Doug. "Is there any circumstance where this kind of tampering wouldn't lead to an accident?"

He laughed. "Uh, no. It's not going to give way while the truck is parked in the garage. If it's moving, and that tie rod goes, you lose control of the vehicle. That means going off the road, or hitting another car. Maybe if you're really lucky, you manage to get it to a complete stop before you hit something or end up in a ditch, but if you're that lucky you should be buying some lottery tickets."

"So there was definitely intent to harm, but was it intent to disable the vehicle and cause an inconvenience, or to injure the driver, or to kill him?" I asked, because I'd seen enough cases come through the office on our bail clients that

I knew if this ever went to court, the prosecutor would have to at least prove intent to harm if they wanted more than a manslaughter conviction.

"Murder? Probably not murder," Doug replied. "Definitely intent to wreck the car, and I'd say intent to injure, since the wreck would likely be serious enough to result in cuts and bruises at least. Beyond that…with air bags and seat belts and crumple zones the way they are on these newer vehicles, I'd say this wasn't the way to go if you wanted someone dead."

"But there's always that chance…." I thought out loud.

"Oh yeah, always that chance. If that tie rod broke clipping the curb while parking or hitting a pothole on Main Street, then he probably would have walked away with a few bruises at most. I can't think whoever did this would have known it would break while going fifty around a sharp curve on a road lined with trees and ditches."

Maybe. Or maybe not. If the sabotage had happened during whatever party Holt had been at late Monday night, then maybe whoever did this knew Holt would most likely take the Jones Road short cut going home, and that he tended to drive faster and more aggressively than he should. Although that was a long shot of a theory. More likely someone was pissed at Holt Dupree and decided a few bruises and a wrecked truck would do him some good.

Miles stared down at his notepad. "Don't do anything further on this truck, Doug. I'll let you know when you can send it off to be crushed, but until then hang on to it. And for God's sake, don't tell anyone about this, okay?"

Doug's chest puffed out, and he beamed. "Will do, Deputy Pickford."

I pulled my notebook from my pocket as Miles and I headed out of the salvage yard. "Do you want to see my suspect list?"

The officer stopped so abruptly that I nearly ran into him. "What are you doing, Kay? Is J.T. investigating this for Holt's mother for a wrongful death suit? Or for the insurance company? He didn't mention anything to me this morning, but there has to be some reason you were out here at Doug's looking at his truck."

J.T. didn't blab about every client we had. He was a gossip, but he understood the need for confidentiality, even if he bent privacy expectations quite a bit in his YouTube videos. All I needed to do was tell Miles this was for an unnamed client, and refuse to elaborate further. But I hated to lie.

"It's not a case. Peony is one of Madison's friends and I'm looking into this for her."

"Well you don't need to look into it further." Miles suddenly put on his cop-face, and although he was more than thirty years younger than me, I felt like a child who'd been caught stealing candy from the corner store.

"So you'll interview these people?" I tore the page out of my notepad and tried to hand it to him.

"No, I'll talk to a few people and try to get an idea of what Holt was doing for the last two days of his life so I can figure out where and when the truck was tampered with."

"And *who*," I pushed the list toward him once more.

He still had his stern, cop-face on. "Maybe, if I get the go-ahead from work to pursue this."

"Why wouldn't you get the go-ahead?" I demanded, still holding the outstretched paper. Yes, the cop-face intimidated me, but I was determined to persist, refusing to let a man young enough to be my son cower me into silence and inaction.

Miles sighed in frustration. "Because this is all most likely a civil matter, Kay. It's something Holt's mother will use to fight the insurance company to get them to pay full benefits even if it turns out Holt was drunk. It's something she'll use to bring civil suit against whoever sabotaged the car. You heard Doug. The intent here wasn't murder, and I'm not even sure how much this contributed to Holt's death."

"How can you say that?" I demanded. "At the very least it's vandalism and assault. And even if Holt was drunk, he might have gotten home safe if that tie rod hadn't failed along the way. The tie rod being tampered with caused the accident. It was a contributor to his death, if not the cause of it. That's got to be good for at least a manslaughter charge if not second-degree murder."

"This is Holt Dupree," Miles countered. "He was a celebrity. His death is all over the news. There's no way the big brass is going to want to stir up the kind of attention a bogus murder charge will cause. The chances of conviction on something like this are slim to none. The DA's office isn't going to want to take a case where they have to argue whether the primary cause of the accident was Holt being drunk or because his truck was messed with."

"You don't know for sure he was drunk," I shot back. From Miles's expression, I was pretty sure I had the sixty-year-old-widow version of his cop-face on right now.

"He. Was. Drunk. And when we get the labs back and the M.E. finalizes the report, you'll see that I'm right." Miles ran a hand through his buzzed hair. "Kay, I've seen hundreds of drunk driving accidents in my career. I've been first on the scene more times than I want to remember. I've held people's hands as they've died, waiting for the bus to arrive. I know an 'under the influence' wreck when I see one. I get that you want to help your friend, but you're not a detective. You're not a private investigator."

His words stung more than I cared to admit. Was I really just a gossipy old lady playing at being a sleuth? Did he see me as an eccentric fool, sticking her nose in where it didn't belong? "No I'm not a private investigator, I'm just a woman who witnessed a fatal car accident, a woman who wants to see justice done."

The cop-face faded, and suddenly Miles was just a tired man in a uniform, standing in the parking lot of a salvage yard next to his cruiser. "Justice is what we all want, Kay. But sometimes we get something different, and that needs to suffice."

Maybe for him, but not for me.

# CHAPTER 19

*I* found Kendra's number through her social media accounts, and surprisingly she was willing to meet with me after work. I guess I wasn't the only one in town who loved gossip because the gorgeous redhead had barely sat down with her chai latte before she started grilling me about the details of Holt's accident. I would have thought she'd be upset rather than excited over the death of a guy she'd spent the last weekend sleeping with, but that wasn't the case.

"Everyone thought you'd be heading off with Holt for pre-season training." That seemed like a good lead-in to my questions, even though the comment sounded a bit odd coming after her insistence on knowing all the gory details of Holt's death.

She scowled. "I'd hoped so, although I knew it was a long shot. I wasn't a one-night stand. He was pretty much with me all weekend. I was expecting him to offer, but Monday night I got the 'it's been fun' speech. Jerk."

Monday night. Although I couldn't see Kendra as the type of woman who would be crawling underneath a pickup truck with a cutting torch in hand. "Did you guys go to the fireworks Monday night?"

She nodded. "Yeah. We almost didn't make it in time because after the parade, Holt and I went back to my apartment for some fun, you know. He had to drive like a maniac to get to the carnival grounds in time. I thought we were going to have to park way out by the grocery store, but one of the parking guys recognized Holt and waved him to one of the handicapped spaces in the lot."

I really didn't want to contemplate what sort of activities they'd been doing to lose track of time for twelve hours.

Drove like a maniac. That meant it was unlikely the tie rod had been damaged before the carnival. And if Holt had parked in a handicapped space, he would have been in the gravel lot where the sparklers were—a perfect spot for sabotage.

"And you guys were there until the fireworks ended?"

"Yeah. Then we went to the party. Well, first we pulled off in this field and got frisky, then I made Holt run by the liquor store, then we went to the party." Her eyes sparkled at the thought. She might not be terribly broken up about Holt's death, but it was clear she'd enjoyed being with him. And enjoyed *being* with him as well. Sheesh, how many times *had* they done it that day? Although when Eli and I had been young, we'd probably been the same.

Wait. Liquor store? "What did Holt buy at the liquor store?"

She sniffed. "A six-pack of those canned margaritas for me. Oh, and a bottle of whisky for me to take home since he was buying. Holt didn't drink. Thankfully he didn't mind that I did. Wish I hadn't left the whisky in his car, but I didn't think that he was going to dump me and not drive me home."

"He left you stranded at the party?" I was outraged, even though this woman was as shallow as a saucer. At least I knew where the bottle of whisky had come from, although Miles would no doubt counter that Holt probably took a few swigs out of it when no one was looking.

"Well...he didn't exactly leave me stranded," she confessed. "We fought because he'd been talking to that Smith girl, then when he told me that I was just a weekend fling, I threw my canned margarita at him and left."

The visual of her throwing a canned margarita at Holt was amusing. "So you walked home? Hitched a ride? Was the party near your house or something?"

Kendra gave me that look that young women give older women who have uttered something completely out of touch with modern times. "No. Duh. David drove me home."

I *was* completely out of touch with modern times. "Your ex-boyfriend David? You dump him and spend the whole weekend between the sheets with Holt Dupree, then a few days later, after you've been rubbing his nose in your new fling, you stomp off in a huff and get the guy to drive you home."

"He's not my ex-boyfriend," Kendra said, outraged. "I never dumped David. I mean, if Holt had asked me to come with him, then I would have dumped David, but that didn't happen. We were just on a break. And when Holt gave me the shove, right in front of everyone too, the break was over."

Had David tampered with Holt's pickup before all this had gone down in revenge for being made a cuckold? If so, then he would have been taking the risk that Kendra would have been hurt, or possibly killed in the accident as well. Or maybe after being publicly humiliated, Kendra had convinced her not-ex-boyfriend to do an act of revenge on Holt's truck.

"What time did you and David leave?"

She wrinkled her nose. "One? Two? It was late and we were really drunk."

"And Holt left at the same time? To drive Peony Smith home?"

She laughed. "Holt was still there when we left, but he wasn't with that kid Peony. He was with Violet."

\* \* \*

HOLT HAD BEEN WITH VIOLET—HIS girlfriend from back in high school, the one, judging from the expression on his face at the concert, that he'd never fallen out of love with. It didn't really have any bearing on my unofficial investigation. Violet didn't have any motive that I knew of to wish Holt harm, and I couldn't see her crawling under a truck to tamper with a tie rod any more than I could see Kendra doing that. I did note her name though, just in case I needed information on what happened after Kendra and David left the party.

It was dinnertime, and I didn't really have a good excuse to go interview David Tripp, but Kendra had helpfully shared that he was on shift at the firehouse tonight, so I drove over there, hoping for the best. A fireman, tossed aside for a weekend fling with a football star only to take Kendra back when her plans for her new beau hadn't panned out. It was a humiliating situation for any guy, but I could imagine the scorn would be far worse for a fireman.

I had no idea what David Tripp looked like, but the friendly captain at the firehouse called him over, then stood next to three other guys obviously curious what a sixty-year-old woman would want with their buddy. I was assuming that David had suffered enough, and asked him to come outside, claiming that I needed to talk to him about a part in J.T.'s reality YouTube series.

He came out of a back room, the sort of fireman who should be gracing the covers of a romance novel. David was Chippendales-dancer hot with light brown wavy hair and sexy stubble on his chiseled jaw. Sultry blue eyes gave me a once-over, then he smiled and I felt a bit weak at the knees.

Kendra ditched *this* for Holt Dupree? Correction, Kendra went on a break? Holt had been a good-looking guy, but David was breathtaking. I guessed in Kendra's eyes, money had a higher value than drop-dead gorgeous looks.

"I spoke with Kendra a little bit ago and she told me you gave her a ride home from the party Monday night." I jumped right in without any preamble because it was getting late and I was hungry, a bit flustered by this smoking-hot fireman, and quite honestly I wasn't sure how to ease into this as I'd done with Kendra.

"Is Gator doing a show on Holt Dupree's accident? That's so cool!" David straightened his shoulders and assumed a serious, camera-worthy expression that made me feel on the edge of a swoon. "Yes, I drove Kendra home about one in the morning. She'd had a huge fight with Holt Dupree, thrown a can of beer at him, and dumped him. She told him she never wanted to see him again, that she was going back to me."

It wasn't beer. And Kendra didn't dump Holt.

"That's not what she told me. That's not what the others at the party are likely to say either."

He deflated before my eyes. "Can we not put that in the video? I mean, yeah he crooked his finger and Kendra came running. He's a celebrity. He's got an NFL contract. I just cleared my probation period as a small-town firefighter. Of course she's going to give it a shot and see if she can hit the big time with Holt."

I had never in my life known a man to rationalize being dumped in such a logical, unemotional way, so I raised an eyebrow and waited.

"Okay, yeah I was mad. She's been my girl for a year now and suddenly she chucks me aside for some dude who she knows is going to dump her after a night or two? It's embarrassing."

"I'll bet you *were* angry with Holt, blowing into town and taking away your girlfriend like that." I commented.

He snorted. "No. I was mad at Kendra. Can't blame a guy for wanting a piece of that. I mean, look at her. But we were exclusive. We'd been together a year."

"At least she didn't sneak around behind your back."

"She could hardly do that if she wanted to be more than a one-night thing with Holt," David commented reasonably. "She wanted more. She was like glue to him from that party on Persimmon Bridge until the fight Monday night. Wouldn't return my calls or texts or anything."

He had motive, although he didn't really seem all that angry with Holt. I'm sure he had enough knowledge about vehicles from his job as well as access to the equipment to cut through a tie rod end, though.

"So tell me about the party," I asked, figuring if I confronted him directly, he'd clam up and I'd get nothing.

"I got there after the fireworks and had a few beers. Was eyeing up some girl from Milford when Holt and Kendra arrived. I didn't expect they'd be going, and thought about leaving when I saw them." David scowled. "She was hanging on his arm, her hair all messed and her lipstick freshly touched up. After a year together, I know what Kendra looks like when she's been getting some. I really didn't want to be there with them, if you know what I mean, but I'd had a couple beers and needed to wait before I drove home. Besides it was a big party and I just kinda stayed out of their way."

"But Kendra knew you were there."

His expression turned dreamy, with a sappy little smile. "Yeah, she did. Holt was talking to that girl he grew up with, the one he dated back in high school who isn't really that hot, especially compared to Kendra. He was just talking to her, but Kendra likes to have a guy's full attention, so she said something to him. They fought. And yeah, he told her she was just a good time for the weekend and to not get any ideas. She started screaming and threw her drink at him then stormed off."

"And went right to you."

The smile got even sappier. "Yeah, right to me. It had been a couple hours and I hadn't had anything else to drink, so I took her home. And I showed her how a man should be treating a smoking hot babe like her."

Eww. It was clear to me that David would have never risked Kendra's safety, or beautiful face, by tampering with Holt's truck pre-argument, and I got the feeling that after the fight he was more interested in dragging Kendra off and proving his devotion than in taking the time to stick it to the guy who'd dumped her. I was pretty confident in crossing David off my suspect list.

But maybe he'd seen something. He and Kendra had left before Holt, and it was looking like the sabotage had been done at the party.

"Where were you parked? Were you anywhere near Holt's truck?"

He blinked in surprise, the sappy smile fading a bit. "Yeah, I guess. We were all parked by the garages and next to the loaders and pavers. They'd moved all the equipment aside and there was a ton of space."

Loaders and pavers? "Where was this party? Who was giving it?"

"Buck Stanford. Not at his house, but at the paving company shop in the field back behind the buildings and storage areas. It was a huge party—bonfire, more fireworks, even a DJ. Kegs all over the place."

"Why would Buck Stanford invite Holt Dupree to his

party?" I asked. "Unless he crashed it. Do you think he crashed it?"

"Wouldn't put it past him. That's why I was so surprised when Kendra and Holt showed up. I thought Buck would kick him out, or maybe there'd be another fight like there was after the concert. Guess they worked it out though, because Buck went over and said 'Hi' to Holt. Even gave him a beer. I'm not saying he was all buddy-buddy with the guy, but he wasn't running him off his property with a shotgun either."

I suddenly had a new top suspect.

"Did Holt drink the beer?" I asked, mostly to myself.

David laughed. "He gave it to Kendra. I gotta say the whole weekend, any time I saw Holt Dupree, he was never drinking alcohol. Pretty much all he had was bottled water, and he drank that stuff by the caseload from what I could tell. Don't blame him with that NFL contract. Guy can't be too careful when there's millions riding on his being able to intercept a pass."

"So it seems unlikely that Holt's accident was alcohol related?"

"I mean, the guy could have been sneaking a few drinks late at night when there was no one around to see. Can't rule that out. But in my opinion, I think he just judged that curve wrong. I can't tell you how many serious accidents we respond to on that road, in that same exact spot. It's a dangerous curve."

It was. And even more dangerous if someone had sliced almost through the tie rod of your truck.

CHAPTER 20

*B*uck wasn't at the Stanford Paving offices, so I left a message for him to call me and took a quick peek around while I was there. There was a section of flattened ground with the remains of a large bonfire and a few stray beer cans in the back. I stood by the charcoaled logs and looked to where the parking area would have been. The buildings and the heavy equipment blocked most of my view. Partiers wouldn't have had a clear view of their cars, or the ability to see someone taking a cutting torch to one of them. There would still be a risk that someone would head back to grab a sweater or another six pack of beer and see, but it might not be huge risk with the equipment and other cars in the way.

A shadow formed just off to my left.

"I'm working on it. Be patient, okay?"

The ghost shifted, and a charcoaled log rolled off the stack then lurched forward shedding bits of black ash.

"Kicking logs isn't going to bring you back to life or help us send whoever tampered with your pickup to jail."

The log launched a few feet forward. This was starting to

147

scare me. Seeing dead people was bad enough without them shoving things off counters and kicking things. I turned to face the ghost but it moved, staying in my peripheral vision.

"Go away. Go away or I'm calling Olive."

Without waiting to see if my threat had any effect, I spun around and stomped off, waiting for a charcoaled log to whack the back of my head. It didn't. So either Holt was gone, or he'd never practiced punting during his years in football.

Heading back, I walked the parking area, trying to hurry before someone from the paving company showed up to ask me what the heck I was doing. The receptionist hadn't seemed all that interested in anything that didn't involve her cell phone, and it was after hours. Hopefully no late-working employee would catch me.

Hopefully Buck Stanford wouldn't catch me. I was getting an uneasy feeling about this whole not-a-case. If it was Buck who'd tampered with Holt's car, I didn't really want to confront him. No, leave that to the police. I'd had enough of brushes with murderous criminals in the last few months.

Right by a huge pile of gravel I found it. Holt and Kendra had arrived late due to their field-frolics and pit-stop at the liquor store, and the paved parking area closer to the party was already filled according to David. Out by the entrance was a section of packed dirt where the company stored the asphalt and stone for their work. There was a spot with sparse flattened grass and tire tracks, and a portion where it looked like fireworks had been set off—fireworks or perhaps sparks from a cutting torch.

I'd gone as far as I could. I wasn't a licensed private investigator, and I certainly wasn't the police, so I got in my car, picked up the phone and called Miles. And when he answered, I dumped the whole mess in his lap.

\* \* \*

"Good Lord, Kay, I was about to send the cavalry after you," Judge Beck commented as I came through the door.

I dumped my laptop and purse on the table and bent to pick up Taco, who was meowing insistently and weaving around my legs.

"He's lying," Judge Beck told me. "I fed him half an hour ago. He wouldn't leave me alone. Kept jumping on my lap and meowing in my face. He thinks he's starving, you know."

"He's always hungry." I bent my head so Taco could bump my forehead with his and rub his face along mine as he purred. Little fattie. It was hard to resist giving him treats when he was so adorably affectionate.

"Well I was hungry too. There's leftover mac and cheese in the fridge."

My stomach growled at the thought and I headed to the kitchen. "Come with me. I've got a million things to tell you. Holt Dupree's truck was tampered with—tampered with enough for him to lose control and wreck."

I told the judge the whole story while I warmed up the mac and cheese and was gratified by his astonished expression.

"So you think it's Buck Stanford?" He frowned. "There's not enough there to bring charges against him, you know that, right? Motive and opportunity do not make for a solid indictment case. Now if someone saw him, or heard him threaten to do it…"

I put up a hand. "I know, I know. I called Miles Pickford and gave him what I'd found out from Kendra and David and what I'd seen at the paving company. He's in a better position than me to scour the town for witnesses and build a case."

He was in a better position than me if Buck was our

culprit and decided he wanted to shoot or stab the person investigating Holt Dupree's death.

The judge's smile held more than a hint of relief. "Good. Let him handle it. For all we know, Buck is innocent and someone else messed with Holt's car."

"There aren't that many suspects who had motive, knowledge, and the ability to take a cutting torch to a tie rod underneath a truck. Heck, before today I didn't even know what a tie rod was. And don't ask me to crawl under a car and point to one, because I'm pretty sure I'd get it wrong."

"So you thought either David or Buck, but who's to say one of the other suspects isn't a secret mechanic. Lots of women work on their own cars nowadays. We're in an age of equal opportunity, you know."

He was teasing, but I couldn't help grin at the thought of Kendra Witt crawling under a truck to torch the suspension system. If that woman wanted to kill someone she'd use a knife, or a canned margarita, and it would be in the heat of passion. Violet or Peony might know enough about cars to do it based on their background, but neither one had reason to want Holt Dupree dead—especially Peony who was in the truck at the time of the accident.

"I'll admit for a moment I thought it might be Ashley Chen's dad. Or Swirly Maury."

He laughed. "Okay, I have no idea who Swirly Maury is, but *Robert Chen*? If you had ever met the guy, you would realize how ridiculous that idea is. The man's pajamas probably have knife-pleat presses in them. His t-shirts are probably starched and ironed. I've never seen him with so much as a spot of mustard on his tie. I'm pretty sure he puts a bib on before he even drinks his coffee. There's no way Robert Chen would drive out to a party behind a paving company, then crawl under a truck with a cutting torch. If Robert wanted to hurt Holt Dupree, he'd dredge up that whole business with the texts and pictures from high school and scare off any big-deal contracts who might want Holt to be the face of their next sport drink or jogging shoes, not tamper with his truck."

He had a point. Yes, Robert Chen might have hired someone to do his dirty work for him, but if Judge Beck said it wasn't the guy's style, then it wasn't. Besides, Buck Stanford was the much better suspect at this point. But the judge's comments did bring a question to my mind.

"Why didn't Robert Chen do all that when everything happened with Ashley back in high school?" I asked. "Why not sue Holt, or find some way of making him and his family's life so miserable that he had to leave town? Isn't that what rich people do when someone wrongs them? Throw lawyers and bury someone in a legal mess?"

Judge Beck shot me a narrow look. "Yes, that's what a lot of rich people do, but not Robert. First, they were all kids, and although Holt had done something horrible, he was still a teenager. Bullying a teenager and his family isn't Robert's style. And then he had his daughter to think about. Ashley has been in treatment for depression and other mental health issues since she was a child. She was fragile then. She's still fragile. Robert's primary concern was to get her safely away from the scandal, somewhere she could heal and recover. He wanted it all to die down and be buried forever, not rake it all up again."

"If that had been Madison?" I asked.

"Madison would have punched Holt in the face, rallied her friends around her for support and faced it down, then come home and cried on my shoulder. But Madison doesn't live with the demons that Ashley Chen does. And I'm not Robert." A steely glint flashed in the judge's eyes then died. "Actually I would have done the same as Robert. As much as I would have wanted to crush the boy that hurt my daughter, I wouldn't have wanted the shame and scandal exacerbated by lawsuits and arrests. Although I would have been tempted to do something sneaky in revenge."

"But not six years afterward."

He sighed. "No, not six years afterward."

"Well then, Robert Chen is out. And I'm pretty sure Swirly Maury is out. And I know Kendra Witt is out. That leaves David Tripp and Buck Stanford, and my money is on Buck Stanford."

"In the conservatory with a candlestick?" Judge Beck teased.

The microwaved dinged and I took out my mac and cheese. "No, in the parking lot of Stanford Paving with a cutting torch."

# CHAPTER 21

*M*iles met me at work the next morning, and this time he was the one who brought pastries. They might have been a box of glazed donuts from the gas station quick-mart down the street, but I appreciated the gesture.

"I passed everything over to the detective last night," he told me as he handed me a donut. "All my notes on what you found out as well as a statement from Doug at the tow yard and pictures of where the tie rod was cut through. They think there's enough to look at this as a potential homicide, even if Holt was drunk."

"Judge Beck says there's not enough for an indictment," I warned him.

He nodded, stuffing half a donut in his mouth. "No, but there's proof of tampering, and it's strong enough to make the argument that Holt Dupree wouldn't have wrecked if his truck hadn't been messed with. Hopefully his blood alcohol level won't be too high. You can be a witness that although he was driving fast, he wasn't weaving all over the road, and was in control of the vehicle until the tie rod went."

I wrinkled my nose because I had no idea exactly when that tie rod had failed. Hopefully there would be an expert they could put on the stand for that one.

"So will I be seeing an arrest for Buck Stanford in the papers sometime soon?"

"Hopefully you'll be seeing an arrest of someone sometime soon, but it's too soon to say anything besides the fact that several individuals are persons of interest in the case."

"It's going to be hard to prove Buck did it," I lamented. "I'm sure there are cutting torches at the paving company, and it wouldn't be a big deal for his prints to be on them. Even the scorch marks in the grass can be explained as part of their normal business operations."

"Somebody saw something," Miles said confidently. "They just didn't realize it, or know what they were seeing. I'm sure someone at that party saw Buck, or whoever, dragging a cutting torch out of one of the garages, or saw someone crawling out from under Holt's truck. Maybe we'll get lucky and he bragged to one of his friends, or got careless and burned a hole in his shirt, or got snapped in the background of someone's selfie. Holt was a big deal in this town. Once the word goes out that we're looking for someone who tampered with his truck at the party, someone will come forward."

I believed him. David was excited for his fifteen minutes of fame, and so were Kendra and the others. Someone out there would be thrilled to have their picture in the paper, or their interview on J.T.'s show, as the guy who helped catch Holt Dupree's killer.

It might end up as a manslaughter conviction, but I still considered it murder.

"What can I tell Peony?" I asked Miles. "I don't want to screw up your case, but she left a message last night and is pushing me for an update. I really want to be able to at least tell her she was right about something being wrong with the truck."

"Keep it general," Miles warned. "Just let her know for now that there was something wrong with the truck and that the police are investigating it. Don't let her know that you consider Buck a suspect. We'll want to interview her again since she was at that party. Hopefully she saw something."

I nodded, wanting to make sure this all went off without a hitch. I didn't think Buck Stanford was the kind of guy to flee the state, but if he had any inkling that the police were coming after him, he might hide or destroy evidence.

"Will do. I'll meet with Peony this afternoon and let her know."

Miles saluted me with a donut. "Sounds good. And, Kay? If you ever want a change in careers, the academy is always looking for good lady cops."

I laughed because I doubted the police academy would be approving an application from a sixty-year-old woman. But Miles's comment brought to mind something I'd been thinking about the last few days.

"Actually, I'm thinking of getting my P.I. license. Maybe J.T. could use me for more than just skip tracing."

Miles grinned. "Absolutely. Then his show can be Gator and Gatorette, Private Investigators."

I'd had enough of cameos in J.T.'s YouTube videos. No way was I going to star in any of them.

"Uh, no. That is not going to happen," I told Miles.

The deputy left the donuts behind, and I helped myself to two more, practically vibrating with the sugar high as I pulled credit reports and ran arrest records. Holt's ghost appeared once more. I ignored him as he tossed a few file folders on the floor and tipped over the trash can next to J.T.'s desk. When he started kicking one of the filing cabinets, I stuck my earbuds in and kept working, hoping that they arrested somebody soon for the truck sabotage. This ghost's poltergeist activities were annoying the heck out of me, and I wanted him gone. Two days. Two days and if there wasn't an arrest, I was calling Olive.

The ghost was gone by lunchtime. I righted the trashcan and picked up the file folders before heading out to the coffee shop to meet Peony. The July heat had ramped up and even with the air conditioning in my car, I was sticky with sweat by the time I got to the coffee shop. Peony waved at me from a table over in the corner, but I headed to the counter and got two frozen mochas, sliding one over to Peony as I sat across from her.

"So I can't tell you any details, but rest assured that the police are investigating. And you were right—something was wrong with the truck. If you hadn't brought that up, I don't think anyone would have checked."

My words didn't do much to reassure the girl across from me. Peony played with the cardboard sleeve on her coffee cup, her other arm in its cast resting on the table.

"Should I get a lawyer?" Her voice was tense. "If someone messed with the truck maybe I could sue them for endangering me."

I stared at her a minute, perplexed by her question. "Holt's insurance company should take care of your medical bills. Is that what you're worried about?"

"I was going to have money. I was going to have lots of money, and they ruined it for me. Holt was going to make me rich, but now he's dead and someone is to blame. I want to know if I have any recourse." Her shoulders slumped. "Probably not. I should have known. My one chance and it's gone. I'll never get a chance like that again."

I had no idea what she was talking about. "Peony, I'm not a lawyer. I suggest you wait until the M.E. gives a definitive cause of death and the police wrap up their investigation, then if you think you have something, go talk to a lawyer."

She nodded, her hair falling forward to drape across the cast.

"How was Holt going to make you rich?" I asked, wondering if they'd concocted a scheme of some sort. Holt hadn't seemed all that bothered with Peony this weekend. Yes, they grew up in the same neighborhood and he used to date her sister, but I didn't get the indication that they were close enough to be working on a project. Holt had been all about Holt. I couldn't see him doing anything to lift a fifteen-year-old girl out of poverty, even one he'd grown up with.

"He always said I looked just like Violet, that I looked exactly like she had at my age, then he'd get this sappy expression. He still loves her, you know. She was stupid and broke up with him, but even though she dumped him, he still loves her. At the party he asked her to come with him, said he'd marry her and she wouldn't have to drive that old rust bucket or worry about her student loans or work in some stupid office all day for crappy money. He was going to give her everything even after all these years, even after she'd dumped him back in high school. She could have had everything."

I caught my breath and reached out a hand to gently touch Peony's cast. Oh, poor Violet! Engaged, only to lose her fiancé hours later. But why had it been Peony in the truck that night and not Violet? And although I'd seen affection in the girl's eyes after the concert in the park, I hadn't seen love. But she wouldn't have been the first girl to mistake affection and nostalgia for love. Or the first girl to let the promise of a life of ease and riches weigh in her decision making.

"Your sister was going to take you with her, but now that Holt's gone... I'm so sorry Peony."

Her eyes flashed up at mine, and I saw they sparkled with tears. "No! She turned him down. Stupid idiot! She could have had it all but she turned him down. Gave him a hug and told him they couldn't revive the past or some crap like that. How could she say 'no'? How could she?"

I was so confused. "But you said Holt was going to make you rich. If your sister turned him down, then how was he going to make you rich?"

Her mouth set in a stubborn line. "He wanted Violet and couldn't have her, but I look just like her. He told me I looked just like her. And *I'm* not stupid enough to turn him down."

A chill ran through me. "Peony, you're fifteen. And although you might look like your sister did at your age, you're not her. I didn't know Holt Dupree that well, but I don't think he would have risked his entire career to marry an underage girl just because she bears a resemblance to a childhood love."

"We would have kept it quiet until next month when I'm sixteen," she argued. "It's not against the law once I'm sixteen."

"It still would have harmed his career," I told her. "Football fans across America aren't going to support someone who takes a child bride, legal or not."

"Of course they will. They don't care about players who beat their girlfriends, or who beat up reporters, or drive drunk. They don't care about players who run dog fighting rings, or do drugs. As long as they play well and win the game, they're heroes."

"That's not true," I replied, wondering about the use of continuing this argument with a girl who was clearly going to believe what she believed, regardless of what I said. "Those players lost sponsorship contracts, lost playing time, some of them lost their jobs entirely. Holt knew that. You said it yourself about him not drinking. And from what I've been told, he was very careful about not crossing the line with anyone even close to being underage. Peony, I know you're hurt and grieving, and that you're angry that Violet didn't say 'yes' and take you off with her to live in a big mansion, but Holt was not going to risk everything he'd worked so hard for to be with a girl who just looked like someone he loved."

"He would have." That stone set was back in her jaw again, her expression making her seem much older than her fifteen years. "But now he's dead."

I sighed. "Peony, you're welcome to talk to a lawyer, but I really don't think you have any sort of civil case here. Your injuries weren't severe enough to claim permanent disability as a result of the accident, and you're not in a position to put forth a wrongful death claim. That would be his next of kin —his mother."

"I know." Tears left tracks in her make-up as they rolled down her cheek. "I know. I just… I thought that I had a chance. I thought something was finally going to go my way. I'd get out of Trenslertown, never have to worry about a thing the rest of my life."

Maybe she was right. Maybe in his grief over losing Violet, Holt would have settled for the little sister who looked just like her. It would have been like a fairy tale come true for Peony for a few weeks or months, but then she would have found herself cast off just like Kendra.

She'd dodged a bullet. Holt's death had stopped them from something that, whether it affected Holt's career or not, would have only ended in sorrow for Peony. His death might seem like the end of an opportunity for her, but I liked to think it saved her, that it gave her a chance to have a better future—one like her sister Violet would hopefully have.

Peony wiped her tears with the back of her hand. "Thank you for helping me. Madison was right. You're smart, and you're nice. And I really appreciate you helping me."

It was genuine. And I was touched.

"They'll find who did it, Peony. The police will get justice for Holt." I reached out again and touched her cast. "And I'm so glad you survived that accident. You've got your whole life ahead of you. Your whole life."

Her smile wobbled. I got the feeling my words were small consolation. In her mind she'd missed out on a pro-football player and a fortune, and nothing I said was going to make her feel any better about that.

## CHAPTER 22

$\mathcal{V}$iolet Smith sat across from me, her hands folded neatly in her lap. She was wearing a navy blue skirt and a short-sleeve, button down striped shirt. Her blonde hair was in a neat, low ponytail, her make-up understated, her only jewelry a thin silver chain. It all made her look young, like the girl next door was playing dress-up for mock interviews in high school.

"I appreciate this, Mrs. Carrera." Her voice held a slight country-girl drawl that she was obviously trying to smooth out. "I don't have many references outside of my professors at college."

Daisy had been pestering me to help her with mock interviews at the high school next month as part of their career preparedness program, but I was surprised when she asked if I could provide a reference for a recent college grad. I was even more surprised when she told me that college grad was Violet Smith. Daisy thought highly of the girl, and that alone would be worth me writing her a reference on official Pierson Investigative and Recovery Services letterhead, but I was uncomfortable writing a reference when I hadn't even met the girl.

And the interview was a good excuse for me to satisfy my curious nature. Or nosy nature.

I eased back in chair and gave her a reassuring nod. "Why don't we start with you telling me what your major was in college as well as your career aspirations."

Her smile widened, then faltered as she twisted her hands nervously on her lap. "I majored in accounting with a criminal studies minor. I want to get into forensic accounting, but that's not really a job someone gets right out of college, especially someone like me with no experience or connections."

I was already impressed. The girl was well-spoken, clearly had realistic goals and a plan for her future in place. "So what are the steps you'll need to get that job in forensic accounting?"

She told me all about entry-level accounting positions, eventual audit jobs with financial firms, positions that involved research of companies that were declaring bankruptcy, possibly even firms that perform tax audits. As she spoke, she grew animated, her cheeks flushed pink and her hands coming off her lap to wave around emphatically.

"But that's all in the future," she confessed. "Right now I'm trying to get a job at the county tax assessor's office as an assistant. But I don't know anyone in county government."

I didn't either, but I knew people who did, and I was determined to put a bug in their ear about a very promising candidate.

"Well, I'll write up a reference letter for you tonight and e-mail it to you," I told her. "And I know it's none of my business, but how are you doing? I know you and Holt were close."

It was a rotten trick, extending the carrot of a recommendation and attaching a nosy question to it, but Violet didn't seem to mind.

"It's hard," she confessed. "We grew up together. He was my boyfriend back in high school, my first love. It was so good to see him this weekend and catch up. I just can't believe that I'll never see him again."

"Everyone thought you two would end up married," I said.

She laughed. "Who would think that? Besides Holt, I mean, and even that surprised me. We broke up when we were sixteen. I hadn't even heard from him in four years."

"But he still loved you," I pressed.

Her smile turned wistful. "No, I think he missed me. He's been in a world where everyone wants a piece of him, where everyone is trying to climb to success on each other's backs. He's had to put together this public persona, and kick and claw his way to the top, and there's no one in his life that really knows him, that knows who he is inside. There's no one he can trust. That's what I was to him. I'm a childhood friend. I'm someone he could relax around and just be that poor kid from Trenslertown. He thought that was love, but I know better. And I know very well how things would have ended for both of us if I'd married him."

This young woman was wiser than people twice her age. I was pretty sure she was wiser than me.

"Peony never understood why you broke up with him in high school. She didn't understand why you didn't marry him and ride off into the sunset."

The smile vanished from Violet's face. "Peony is just like Holt, you know. I love her, and I really want something different for her, but she's just like Holt. She thinks I'm a fool for running up all this debt and going to college just so I can get an entry-level job and bust my tail for decades working my way up the corporate ladder. She doesn't think anyone from Trenslertown can get out of poverty that way. She thinks the only way out is to be like Holt, to climb out on the backs of other people."

"And that's why you broke up with Holt?" I asked softly. "Because of Buck Stanford?"

Her laugh this time was bitter. "Oh, there were other things before Buck Stanford's 'accident' on the football field, and every one of those things showed me just how ruthless Holt could be. He'd go to any lengths to get what he wanted, and if someone was in his way, they were going to be steam-rolled, or clipped after the play. He wasn't the kid I grew up with anymore, and at fifteen I saw what kind of man he was going to be. I didn't want that. I still don't want that. I'll take that tax assessor's assistant job over being an NFL player's wife any day."

I shook her hand and walked her to the door, promising to e-mail the recommendation tonight and put a hard copy in the mail to her. Then I watched her get in her rust-bucket car and drive off. She'd turned down Holt Dupree. Maybe Peony was right. Maybe in his grief, Holt would have been willing to accept a substitute.

I guess that was something we'd never know.

# CHAPTER 23

"Guess what just came in this morning?" Miles strolled into my office. This was becoming a regular occurrence. The cop and I seemed to have bonded over this Holt Dupree thing, although the both of us were now viewing it from the sidelines.

"Labs?" Thank heaven our local police were such gossips. I'd been curious to know if Holt was drunk or not—and if the M.E. thought he was drunk enough to attribute the accident to alcohol, or the vehicle tampering.

"Labs and cause of death. Guy was sober as a judge. Not even the equivalent of a dose of cough syrup worth of alcohol in him."

"Well, that makes a whole lot more work for your detective. The pressure is going to be on to find who tampered with the truck and 'murdered' Holt Dupree."

"Nope. Guess again."

Miles pulled up a chair, his grin both smug and excited.

"Guess again what? Sober. Loss of control due to sabotage of the vehicle. What's to guess?"

The officer leaned forward. "No alcohol, but Holt *did* have drugs in his system."

My mouth fell open. "Steroids? Holt was on steroids?" I could hardly believe it. "He was an athlete. He had a huge NFL contract. They drug test, don't they? I can't believe he would sabotage a career he'd worked so hard to obtain."

Miles waved his coffee at me. "No, not steroids, drugs. Flunitrazepam."

I blinked. "What?"

"Better known as Rohypnol."

My mouth fell open. "Roofies?" At the word a shadow appeared over by J.T.'s desk. My heart sank. I hadn't seen Holt's ghost since I'd spoken with Peony, and had hoped that his spirit had been satisfied with the discovery of the tampering and moved on.

I guess not. Roofies. Who would have guessed that one?

"And Viagra," Miles added.

What in the world? "Why would a healthy twenty-two-year-old man need to take Viagra?" I turned to the shadow and smirked, feeling the ghost's anger ratcheting up a notch at what must have been an embarrassing reveal.

Miles shook his head. "I know, but it's starting to be a problem with kids in the last few years. Seems even the young guys want to keep going for up to four hours."

That did not sound like fun to me, although Holt had seemed to be all sex all of the time according to Kendra. Maybe that was how he managed to be doing it half a dozen times a day.

"So Holt Dupree had roofies and Viagra in his system?" I shook my head. "Nobody roofies themselves, so someone must have spiked his drink. Or in this case, his water bottle."

The ghost pushed a pen holder off the desk. Miles jumped to his feet at the sound, stared at the pens rolling across the floor, then turned to me.

"Mice." I shrugged. "I'll get J.T. to get an exterminator in this week." Yeah, an exterminator named Olive.

The deputy shot a nervous glance around the floor. I noticed when he sat down, he held his feet a few inches off the floor. How funny. Miles was afraid of mice. I wondered if he was afraid of ghosts as well?

"I'm thinking drugs in the water bottle too," he told me, his gaze shifting between the fallen pens and the top of J.T.'s desk. "Which means we have someone pissed off enough at Holt to tamper with his vehicle, and someone else pissed off enough to drug him."

I shook my head. If the tie rod end hadn't caused the accident, then the drugs eventually would have. "But don't those things take effect pretty quickly? He should have been passed out half a mile from the party if someone drugged him. Unless it wasn't a whole lot?"

"Oh it was a whole lot, and you're right. It takes effect fast. Doesn't mean he didn't down it at the party, though. Someone may have handed him a water bottle they'd laced with roofies, and he spent the evening just carrying it around. I'm guessing he didn't drink it until he was driving home."

I eyed the shadow. For once Holt's ghost wasn't knocking anything over.

"So if the tie rod end hadn't snapped and caused the accident, then he probably would have wrecked another ten miles down the road from the drugs," I mused.

"It would have taken less than one, by my estimate." Miles leaned forward. "Here's the thing—the accident didn't kill Holt Dupree, the drugs did. The M.E. found that he had quite a few injuries from the crash, but nothing that would have caused his death. He died from cardiac arrest. Sometime between when that truck went off the road and the ambulance crew pulled him out of it, Holt stopped breathing and his heart stopped."

I was stunned. "Drug overdose. Someone murdered Holt by drugging him."

The shadow moved closer. A potted plant on top of filing cabinet scooted a few inches, and I glared at the ghost. If that plant hit the floor, I was definitely calling Olive. As if sensing my intentions, the shadow faded and vanished.

Miles leaned back, the smug look returning to his face. "Seems roofies and Viagra are pretty nasty combination, especially in the quantity Holt had in his bloodstream."

"So whoever tampered with his truck isn't the murderer," I mused.

"No, although we still want to press charges if we can find out who did that. The murderer is whoever gave Holt Dupree those drugs." Miles leaned forward again. "We'll find them. And when we do, whoever it is, is going to be spending a very long time in jail."

Drug overdose. I stared down at my files long after Miles had left, trying to think of who would have slipped drugs in Holt's water bottle. It really could have been anyone—any of those millions of spurned girls who were upset Holt wasn't going home with them. It could have been a spiteful act by Kendra right before she left with David. Heck, it could have even been David, or Buck doubling down, or…anyone.

And there was a faint chance that Holt had taken them voluntarily, that he'd mistaken the roofies for the Viagra he'd been popping or some other recreational drug, but it didn't seem likely. The guy who planned every action and word to further his career wouldn't take a chance on recreational drugs. I could see him taking the Viagra. The NFL probably wouldn't have cared one way or another about him trying to enhance his sexual performance. No, those roofies couldn't have been an accident or something Holt would have knowingly taken.

Which left murder. And I had a terrible feeling deep down inside who the murderer might be.

Needing to think, I left the office and once more drove out to Stanford Paving. Buck had never returned my call, but that wasn't the reason for my visit this evening. I just wanted to trace Holt's last steps, to figure out if what I suspected was really what happened.

I sat in the car and thought of Holt arriving late with Kendra after some nookie in the field and a trip to the liquor store. They'd partied. I was sure Holt had grabbed a bottle of water either from the liquor store or at the party, and I couldn't see him carrying it around for a few hours without drinking it, so that bottle must have been clean.

He saw Violet and talked with her. She turned him down. Kendra and Holt fought. She and David left. And I was positive that Holt would have locked his truck so fans didn't loot it, so I doubt Kendra would have been able to spike any bottle of water he had left inside it on her way out.

Holt went to leave, saw Peony walking, and offered her a ride home. No, she'd been there to see him talk with Violet and fight with Kendra. She'd approached him for a ride, made a plan to be Holt's substitute Violet. She wouldn't have just walked off drunk and hoped that Holt would come upon her and offer her a ride. No, she'd planned to seduce him, and she'd approached him at the party, leveraged their childhood friendship as well as her resemblance to her sister to get him to give her a lift home.

And then what? I drove my car along the route Holt would have taken, thinking that it was twenty minutes from Stanford Paving to Trenslertown. Twenty minutes. The roofies would have taken five to ten minutes to take effect.

So halfway home Holt gets drowsy? They pull off the road. And…

That would have left Peony in a truck with a passed-out guy. That hadn't happened, so Holt must have taken the roofies when he was closer to that fatal corner on Jones Road.

I pulled into a diner a few miles from the turn onto Jones Road and went to sit at the counter, ordering a coffee and yanking my notes and files from my briefcase. With them spread out before me, I stared down at the papers. I was pretty sure I knew what happened, but I had no proof. Roofies and Viagra. It was a risky combination. In this case it was a lethal combination. And I truly thought Holt's death was unintentional.

The guy at the counter poured me a coffee and looked down at my open notepad. "That was a real tragedy. I saw him play his senior year. Real talented young man. A gentleman too."

Of all the things that Holt Dupree was, I'd never imagined anyone would ever call him a gentleman. The waiter must have seen my surprise because he chuckled.

"I know. Surprised me too. He came late that night with some young girl and I thought the worst, but he was real kind to her—like a brother. He was trying to sober her up a bit. She tried to get frisky a few times, and he was downright compassionate putting her off and trying to get her to drink her coffee."

"Wait, Holt was in here the night of the Fourth of July?"

He nodded. "Actually the next morning. It was near two o'clock when they left. The girl was a bit more sober. He bought a bottle of water for the road. With all the water the two of them had drank here, you'd think they would have been floating out the door. Nice guy. Tipped well. Real shame he died, but that's a bad curve out there on Jones Road. Easy to cross the center line, especially in the dark."

Peony had never mentioned stopping for breakfast, or for Holt to try to sober her up. With the concussion had she just forgotten it? Or...

"You said they bought a bottle of water for the road?"

He nodded.

"For her?"

He chuckled. "For himself, although she was joking around and snatched it. Said she wanted to take some aspirin or something. He went back to put a tip on the table and she gave it back to him when he came back."

"You saw her take the aspirin?"

"I saw her take a drink then pour something into the bottle. It was a powder. I thought it was one of those lemonade or flavored powders people put in their water sometimes."

Would the drugs have dissolved that fast? They probably would have.

I put some money on the counter and gathered up my files, leaving the untouched coffee. Then once I got to the car, I made a phone call.

I know. I'd sworn I would never put myself in a position where I confronted a murderer again, but this was different. I don't think Peony ever intended to be a murderer, and if she waited for the police to catch her, her future was going to be a whole lot worse than if she came forward on her own and pleaded this out. I might be taking a risk, but I would be in a crowded coffee shop, confronting a fifteen-year-old girl — a fifteen-year-old girl who shouldn't be tried as an adult and have to spend decades in prison, even if she had caused Holt Dupree's death.

# CHAPTER 24

The coffee shop was nearly empty at six o'clock at night. Peony sat in the usual spot off in the corner, her tangled blonde hair covering her face. She was hunched in upon herself, looking so small, so young that I felt a stab of sorrow. Dreading this and wishing I'd just gone to the police, I went to the counter and ordered two frozen mochas.

Yes, I was buying a coffee for a murderer.

Peony looked up at me as I sat down and gave her the coffee. Her crumpled shirt was the same that she'd been wearing yesterday, and I wasn't sure if the dark smudges under her eyes were from old mascara or lack of sleep.

"Did they arrest someone?" she asked after thanking me politely for the mocha.

"No." I took a few sips of my drink at watched her carefully. "But the M.E. ruled on a cause of death."

She stiffened, not meeting my gaze.

"And the labs came back."

The girl froze like a hare in the briars, praying that the fox passes him by.

"They found Viagra in his system."

Her head jerked up, eyes astonished. "Viagra?" She laughed. "Dog! I should have known with all the pu...number of times he was scoring."

"Viagra and Flunitrazepam."

She froze again, the corner of her mouth trembling.

"Roofies." I told her, since she clearly wasn't going to ask what Flunitrazepam was.

Now more than the corner of her mouth was trembling.

"What if Holt had said 'no', Peony?" I asked her. "You knew there was a good chance a sober guy, one who'd just been turned down by the woman he loved wouldn't be satisfied with a fifteen-year-old lookalike. There was a chance he'd lose his judgement and take you up on your offer, but you knew there was a better chance that he'd say 'no'."

Her expression turned wary. "If he'd said 'no' then that would have been that. He would have dropped me off at my house and I never would have seen him again."

"Roofies are commonly date-rape drugs used on women. Fast acting. Difficult to detect in a drink. And they're out of your system fast enough that it's hard to get them to show up on a lab unless the victim gets tested right away. Or dies before their system completely process the drug."

She shoved her hands under the table, and stared at her drink. "You can't date rape a guy with roofies. Girls, yeah. Guys need to get it up, not pass out."

"They wouldn't pass out right away. Just like women, a man who'd been roofied would act like he was really drunk. He'd stumble, slur his speech, be open to suggestion. The passing out would happen later."

Her eyes widened and she took a series of shallow, ragged breaths. "What are you talking about?"

"You knew Holt would probably say 'no' to your seduction attempt. Maybe you wanted a little insurance, just in case. Maybe you had a back-up plan, like slipping something into his water at the diner."

She was silent a moment, then she took a steadying breath and brought her hands back up to hold the mocha. "Holt took me to the diner to sober me up a bit before he took me home. He knew my mom would have a fit, and he didn't want me to show up like that at two in the morning. I was drunk, so I don't remember a lot of it except us drinking coffee and water, and him trying to get me to eat an egg or something. Then we left. I don't know how those roofies got into Holt. Maybe the waiter at the diner did it. Maybe he doesn't like Holt for some reason, or doesn't like football, or the Falcons, or something, but I've got no idea."

"The waiter at the diner saw you slip something into the bottle of water, then hand it to Holt when he came back from paying the tip," I told her.

She was a deer in headlights. I don't even think she was breathing.

"Why, Peony? Why?"

The girl swallowed, lowering her eyes and fidgeting with her drink. "I tried at the diner, but he wasn't interested. He said I was like a little sister to him, even if I did look just like Violet. I thought if he loosened up a little, he'd change his mind."

"And what if he just passed out? What then?"

"I...I thought I could maybe take a few pictures. If Holt didn't want me, then I'd take some pictures of us together and..."

"Blackmail?"

Her eyes met mine, and once again I was struck by how young she seemed. "He was going to have millions. If he just gave me enough to buy a car and move out of my Mom's house. Maybe enough to start up a dog-grooming business or something. It's not like I wanted a fortune or anything. He wouldn't have even missed it with the millions he was going to make."

The similarities between this and Holt sending pictures around of Ashley Chen bloomed in my mind. Violet had been right. Her sister was a lot like Holt. I suddenly realized why Judge Beck was so uneasy about Peony being friends with Madison, and it had nothing to do with her impoverished family. Or maybe it did have a lot to do with her impoverished family. Holt Dupree had dodged a bullet by dying in that car accident, because whether or not he succumbed to nostalgia and heart-break and decided a girl who looked like Violet was good enough for one night, he was going to be faced with a hard decision.

Marry an almost sixteen-year-old girl, or pay up in blackmail money for the rest of his life.

"You need to go down to the police station and confess, Peony. They'll find out. They'll track down the kid at the party that sold them to you. He'll say how you bought them right after Kendra and Holt fought. A kid sold you the drugs, the lab results show those drugs were in Holt's bloodstream at the time of death, and the waiter saw you add them to Holt's water. You're going to be arrested, Peony. The best thing you can do is turn yourself in and confess, and beg for leniency."

Her eyes filled with tears, her face crumbling as she looked at me. Then she sat up straight, and swiped a hand across her cheek. "If that happens, then I'll do some time in juvie for drug possession. Big deal. It's practically a rite of passage in my family. Slipping Holt something in his water shouldn't be what the police are worrying about right now. Someone murdered him. They should be looking for the murderer."

"They are looking for the murderer," I told her gently.

"The murderer is you, Peony. Holt didn't die in the car accident, he died from the drugs you gave him."

She stared at me, her eyes wild. "No! The pickup went crazy. We went off the road. It was a horrible accident. I saw the pictures of the truck. You're wrong. He died of internal injuries, or a head wound. That's what happened."

"No, that's not what happened. He did have injuries, but he should have walked out of the hospital in a few days just like you did. He died of the drugs. Cardiac arrest because of the roofies and the Viagra."

She began to sob. "No! I didn't mean for him to die. He was my friend. We grew up together. I would never have hurt him, never would have killed him. I didn't mean for him to die. I just wanted him, or maybe some money if that didn't work out. It was just roofies. He shouldn't have died from that. I didn't know he was taking Viagra too. I didn't know. I didn't mean for him to die."

He was her friend. She would never have hurt or killed him, just drugged and blackmailed him. He'd died because of her. So why did I feel so sorry for this crying teenager sitting across from me?

"He shouldn't have died," Peony insisted. "Sean said there wouldn't be any lasting effects, that roofied people wake up in the morning and are fine. He didn't say that someone might die. It's Sean's fault. The police should arrest Sean. He's the one that murdered Holt, not me. It was Sean and whoever messed with his truck, not me."

What would need to happen for her to take ownership of what she'd done? I thought about Violet, so hardworking and wise, and Peony ruthless and desperate. How could two girls be so different when they'd grown up exactly the same? Was there something worth saving in Peony? I really didn't know. But I knew Madison liked her. I knew that she'd been dealt a really bad hand in life and was deserving of some kind of second chance. She might have murdered Holt Dupree, but I hated the thought of a fifteen-year-old girl being written off as not worth saving.

Then I thought of what she'd said, about wanting just enough money to get out of her mom's home, buy a car, and start a business—a dog-grooming business. Maybe she was more like Violet than I thought. She just didn't have her older sister's confidence in her own ability to make things happen. I looked at her tear-streaked face, the terrified look in her eyes. She'd need to face this. She needed to find the strength to face this.

"It wasn't Sean that put the drugs in Holt's water," I told her firmly, trying for my best 'mom' tone of voice. "And although the police intend to prosecute whoever tampered with Holt's car, that accident didn't kill him. You did, Peony. You made a horrible mistake. You saw an easy way out of Trenslertown. You gambled with a man's life and lost."

She started to cry again. "Everyone is going to hate me. I killed our local football hero. I killed Holt Dupree. Everyone in town will hate me. My mom will kick me out. Violet will hate me." Peony looked at me, her face red, blotchy, and wet with tears. "Madison will hate me. Her dad will put me in jail. She'll hate me and she's really the only friend I have."

I rose from my chair and held out my hand. "Maybe. Maybe not. But the scandal will die down and you have your whole life to redeem yourself. You still have a chance at a future—at a little apartment, an old car, a dog-grooming business. But you need to take responsibility for your actions. You need to do the right thing, starting now."

She stood and stared at my hand then reached shaking fingers toward mine. "Will you go with me to the police? Will you sit beside me when I talk to them, help me find a lawyer? Will you...will you tell them I'm not a horrible person? That

I didn't mean to kill him? Will you tell Madison that I'm sorry?"

A character reference. I'd be providing one for Violet and a very different one for Peony. I reached out and took her hand, gripping it tight.

"Yes. I'll go with you. And I'll be right by your side if you need me."

# CHAPTER 25

"*I* made a few phone calls. Dennis Rout said he'd take her case pro-bono." Judge Beck ran a hand through his blond hair and grimaced. "Am I a bad person for hoping she goes to jail and vanishes? That I never see her again in my life? That Madison never sees her again in her life?"

"No, you're just a father," I told him. "And you're someone who sees the worst of society every day."

"So do you with your skip traces and bail bond applications. But you still think she's worth saving, that somehow she's going to come out of this and be an asset to society?"

I cringed at the edge of disbelief in his voice. I knew the recidivism rate. I knew that the decks were stacked against Peony, but the decks seemed to be stacked against any kid from Trenslertown. Right then I made a silent vow to help Daisy with her mock interviews, to help Matt with more of his fundraisers. We couldn't just turn our backs on people. We couldn't just write them off when things like this happened. There had to be some way to help people turn their lives around.

"Yes. I know she's worth saving, that she's going to come out of this okay as long as she feels there's something worthwhile once she makes it through."

The judge shook his head. "I'm not the DA, but I think she'll probably be able to plead out with possession and involuntary manslaughter. I don't know what's going to be harder for her: the jail time, or the stigma of being the girl that killed Holt Dupree."

Like a scarlet 'A' forever on her chest—an 'M' for murderer. I winced. "What do you think Madison will do? Peony said she's her only friend."

"I know what I hope Madison will do, but she's got a soft heart like you and your friend Daisy." He hesitated. "And like her mother."

"And like you?" I teased.

His eyes narrowed, but he was on the edge of a smile. "No, not like me. I'm a judge. Soft hearts do you no good in the courtroom."

"The hanging judge then?" I grinned at him. "I've seen your decisions, Judge Beck. Glare at me all you want, but there's a soft heart under those robes."

He grinned back. "Don't tell anyone, okay? I've got a reputation, and I don't want the criminals thinking all they have to do is cry and I'll let them off with a PBJ."

Probation Before Judgement. My smile faded. "How much jail time do you think she'll get?"

The judge shrugged. "Her mom won't post bail, so probably time served up to the plea and possibly another three months."

I thought of Peony having to go back to school after having missed half the year, of how her classmates might react. Then I thought of something else.

"What if her mom kicks her out?"

"There are foster homes, shelters. Your friend Daisy can help her find something. We can force her mom to take her back, but she'll be sixteen and it would probably be easier on her if she asked to be emancipated and got public assistance in housing." Judge Beck sucked in a breath. "Oh no. You're not seriously thinking of letting her live here. No, no, no."

It was an idea. A crazy, reckless idea. I couldn't foster Peony. I had no experience in being a parent, and a teenager like her would be far more than I could handle. Besides, it wouldn't be fair to the judge or his family to foist a troubled girl on them.

"I'll admit I thought about it, but I'd never do that unless you and the kids were totally on board with it."

He shook his head. "I can't, Kay. Not with the divorce and final custody still unresolved. Heather and her lawyer would have a field day if I was living with a convicted murderer."

He was right. But I still worried about Peony, murderer or not.

The judge put his arm around my shoulders and squeezed. "She's got a good lawyer. We'll work with Daisy when she gets out to get her everything she needs to turn her life around. I promise."

It would be okay. Between me and Judge Beck and Daisy, it would all be okay.

"Now let's spread some paperwork across your dining room table and get some work done," the judge continued. "Working dinner tonight. If we finish up early, we can watch some Monty Python movies."

I looked over near the sofa where Eli's ghost hovered, so familiar and reassuring a presence that I almost took him for granted now. Holt's ghost was gone—I hoped gone for good now that Peony had confessed, although I wouldn't be surprised if he stuck around until the police caught who'd tampered with his truck. Hopefully if he came back, he would just float around like Eli did and stop knocking stuff over.

In the meantime I had skip traces to work. Bail bond applicants to research. And I had that application to fill out for my private investigator's license. There would be a background check, and a whole bunch of classes I'd need to take, but J.T. was thrilled at the prospect of expanding his business and my job duties. And hopefully my pay.

It would be a new future for me. But in the meantime I needed to get through the backlog of work that had piled up in the last few days.

I stepped out from under Judge Beck's arm and picked up my files and laptop case. "You microwave the leftovers while I get set up. And when we're done, I've got a batch of cookies to go with our movie tonight."

The judge moved toward the kitchen. "You know, I think these work-and-movie nights are the best ways to end my day."

I plopped my laptop on the dining room table. *Me too. Me too.*

# ACKNOWLEDGMENTS

Special thanks to Lyndsey Lewellen for cover design and typography, and to Jennifer Cosham for copyediting.

## ABOUT THE AUTHOR

Libby Howard lives in a little house in the woods with her sons and two exuberant bloodhounds. She occasionally knits, occasionally bakes, and occasionally manages to do a load of laundry. Most of her writing is done in a bar where she can combine work with people-watching, a decent micro-brew, and a plate of Old Bay wings.

*For more information:*
libbyhowardbooks.com/

ALSO BY LIBBY HOWARD

**Locust Point Mystery Series:**

The Tell All

Junkyard Man

Antique Secrets

Hometown Hero

A Literary Scandal

Root of All Evil

A Grave Situation

Last Supper

A Midnight Clear

Fire and Ice

CPSIA information can be obtained
at www.ICGtesting.com
Printed in the USA
LVHW031136230222
711640LV00001B/29